Learning to Live Indoors

Learning to Live Indoors

Alison Acheson

The Porcupine's Quill

CANADIAN CATALOGUING IN PUBLICATION DATA

Acheson, Alison, 1964–
Learning to live indoors

ISBN 0-88984-201-9

I. Title.

PS8551.C32L42 1998   C813'.54   C98-932480-X
PR9199.3.A23L42 1998

Published by The Porcupine's Quill, 68 Main Street, Erin, Ontario
NOB 1TO. Readied for the press by John Metcalf. Copy edited by
Doris Cowan. Typeset in Ehrhardt, printed on Zephyr Antique Laid,
and bound at The Porcupine's Quill Inc.

The cover, *Inner Weather*,
is after an original intaglio: etching and aquatint by K. Gwen Frank.
The author photo is courtesy of Cleve Hatlelid.

This is a work of fiction. Any resemblance of characters to persons,
living or dead, is purely coincidental.

Represented in Canada by the Literary Press Group.
Trade orders are available from General Distribution Services.

We acknowledge the support of the Canada Council for the Arts
for our publishing programme. The support of the Ontario Arts
Council and the Department of Canadian Heritage through the
Book and Periodical Industry Development Programme is also
gratefully acknowledged.

1   2   3   4   ·   00   99   98

Acknowledgements

I would like to thank those who have encouraged, and have had faith, and have given of their knowledge. In particular, Linda Svendsen, John Metcalf, Leona Gom, Zsuzsi Gartner, and Sue Ann Alderson.

I appreciate the assistance of the Canada Council.

'Learning to Live Indoors' was published in the *New Quarterly*; 'Across the Hall' was published in *Grain*; 'Louis and Me and God and Everyone Else' was published in the *Antigonish Review*.

In memory of Hilda Nuttall
who inspired me to seek and grow

&
for Martin

Contents

Murray Would

THERE WAS ALWAYS a particular routine to that day in November. Jon had known that routine for eight years now. For Karen, his wife, it had been eleven, and she had striven to make it what it was: she'd come to know the value of order. Where there was routine and order, there was a chance for a crude harmony, even some sense of law. She liked to know there was law, even if there was no justice.

She stood outside the shed, balancing the camping coffee pot in one hand, several mugs in the other.

'How about if I don't go this year?' Jon asked, and the mugs clattered to the walk. He couldn't see her face as she stooped to pick them up and examined, with her fingertips, the dents, the chips in the blue-specked enamel.

'Don't go,' she repeated. It wasn't often that he heard that child-like quality in her voice. It pleased him oddly, before he felt anger at himself, before guilt leaked into him, violet-coloured, staining. But he had gone too far.

'Yeah,' he said.

'I've never thought you didn't want to come.' She pushed at a fleck of enamel with her thumbnail. Her nails were wide, as were her fingers, her hands. Jon noticed that the nail was dull purple and lifting at the edges. She'd been persisting at the toolbox then, as she was wont to do. She hadn't mentioned the pain.

'I never would have asked you.' Her voice grew stronger, with a protecting edge. Jon knew that edge. He reminded himself of what it was about, yet when it came to hearing it he heard only the defensiveness, not the fear.

'I never would have asked you,' she repeated, and stood

then, tall and stooped, her legs in slim jeans. He'd first seen her as a cottonwood in the wind, but her roots went deeper, he learned later.

He didn't remind her that she had never asked him to go. It wasn't important.

'It's not that I don't want to go.'

'It's not,' she echoed and looked at him.

Her eyes: *always something missing.*

She put the coffee pot into the box that he held, and the one mug that was fit to drink from. She reached back into the shed for the camping stove.

He spoke to her back. 'There's something I've got to do,' he said, and thought, *What's that? What is it I have to do so badly on this day?*

'Well, Jon,' Karen spoke from inside the shed. 'Do what you have to do.' She passed by him to the pickup and slid the stove over the metal bed of the truck, a loud punctuation to end her words.

This one day that belongs to a dead man.

He went into the house, sat on the basement stairs, untied his hiking boots.

Peter clumped over the floor above. 'Mum! There's not enough hot chocolate! Where's my jacket?' And Elsa: 'We're out of candles for tonight.'

Karen's voice carried into the house. 'Jacket's on the chair where you left it. Candles are in the cupboard.'

Murray would go today.

Peter dragged a chair.

'You're supposed to carry it,' said Elsa, not unkindly.

'Phone the ski report,' he said. 'See if it's pouring. Or icy.'

They spoke as if they were going camping or preparing for a party.

Jon had one sneaker done up. He pulled on the second, tied it too tightly.

It had been a long year, with moments that had stretched out and never quite snapped back, so that the months seemed to have travelled a fitful pace, and now, November again, the year had been too long to return to that same place. They'd almost lost both children. Imagine: a man going from one school to another, hiding in the girls' washroom. Elsa was the second girl, or would have been if that old window hadn't suddenly fallen in its wooden frame. Jon wouldn't think what might have happened. As it was, the bugger ran away and wasn't caught until the third time. That time he didn't have time to run.

Then Peter on his bike, and the truck. A broken collar-bone, and they felt fortunate. At least, Jon did. 'We're so lucky,' he said to Karen, but she got that look on her face. That same look she'd had when they met. *Who's going to take from me now?*

Jon felt there wasn't much he could do about that look. He didn't have that sort of power. He couldn't even tell her what he felt about the window and the truck, and his feeling that someone was looking out for them. Karen thought someone was out to get them. It could appear to be either way, Jon knew.

There'd been a time when he didn't believe in ghosts. Now he wasn't so certain, because of Murray. He lived in Murray's house, with his children, with his wife.

Karen said that they couldn't allow the children to forget him. 'It would be as if he never existed, never was a part of this family.'

'A founding member,' Jon said, his voice lighter than his intent. He'd learned the trickery of the light voice from his mother, a woman who had struggled for years to hew life into an uncomplicated thing. There shouldn't be ghosts between people, she always said, and if there are ghosts, they shouldn't be named. *How about having their own place at the table?* Then Jon felt like a bastard. It wasn't like that, and funny thing was, he knew he would have liked Murray. They probably would have played drop-in hockey together, liked each other's company at neighbourhood barbecues, talked at the convenience store picking up cigarettes or a paper. Funny thing.

November 29 was either wet, cold, or both. The kids who did it – who knocked him down – did they mean to do more? – must have been scared as hell. They must have thought no one would look there, at least not for a long time, but a hiker and his dog discovered Murray's body only a week later.

Karen didn't remember the week after she last saw him. Except she dreamed about it. Couldn't remember anything when she awoke. Probably would have denied her cries, though Jon never pressed her. He found her once crawling through the cedar trees in the side yard and whimpering because her ears hurt with some sound only she could hear.

Danny told Jon that they found her there before: in the week after Murray disappeared a policeman was sent round to check on her. He figured she'd been there since he last saw her. Karen and the trees – it was as if she knew all the time. They found Murray under cedars.

'You going to sit there all day?' Karen looked through the basement door at Jon, still on the bottom stair of raw stained wood.

'No. I've got something to do,' he repeated stupidly. He tried angling his mouth into a particular smile that made her laugh. Not that day, though. His mouth slackened.

She stepped into the basement. 'Are you going to tell the kids that you're not coming with us? Or am I going to tell them?'

'I'll tell the kids.' *I can do that,* he thought, pulled himself to his feet with the handrail, then on up the stairs, slowly. *Like a bloody old person.*

[12]

'Elsa. Peter.' They were standing in the kitchen.

'Yeah, Dad,' said Peter.

Jon remained two steps from the top, still holding the railing. 'I won't be going with you this year.' If he offered a reason, they'd want an explanation. Maybe they wouldn't ask.

'Hey,' he added. 'At least there'll be enough hot cocoa.'

Elsa looked at him and her lips thinned. She went away down the hall and her bedroom door closed. Peter squinted – Jon always told him he needed glasses – then he pushed past on the stairs and shoved at Jon, though the stairway was wide. 'Whatever,' he said, and his words sounded like his mother's. *Do what you have to.*

Jon returned to his place at the foot of the stairs, and he loosened his sneaker; his foot was numb. He could hear Karen and Peter loading the truck, then their feet climbed up the back steps to the porch outside the kitchen. The door closed.

Sometimes when Jon looked at Karen he felt far away, felt as if he couldn't truly know her pain, maybe never even know her. He did know that he could inadvertently cause her more pain. It was a silly wish, but he wished he were deathless. Silly, because it was the wish of a boy dressed in outgrown pyjamas, a tea-towel cape pinned at his throat with a mother's brooch: a tiny hero, fearless on the banister, defiant on the fifth step, jubilant on the landing. As a man he brooded over the mountain, and always before him there was a tree, a tree with a mark so high – he leapt to reach it, tried to climb, but always slid back, fell away.

Karen knew the shadowed corners of loving. He could have asked her, but he didn't; one could have the answers and not live by them. It was a mind and soul thing. His mind said he was loved. His soul was adrift.

The mountain was dark, even when there was snow. Of course, under the cedars there was never much snow. The first year, Karen had told him, there was a crowd, a procession, trailing up the road: the hiker who found Murray's body; one of the detectives – turned out he wanted to get to know Karen; two newspaper photographers; someone from a talk show; some TV producer who pressed his card into Karen's hand. He brought flowers – paid for with the station's petty-cash fund, Karen figured, the receipt in his pocket. They all brought flowers.

Jon was there the fourth year: a test, he felt, after months of cautious intimacies. They watched him, Murray's friends, and they watched Karen, and when it was over, Danny put his big hand at Jon's elbow, and handed him a camping bowl filled with coffee. After that, Jon made the coffee.

Jon inherited Murray's friends, and they were good people, he discovered. Loyal. They brought plants each year, and after the ceremony they dug holes in the earth, planted them. One year everyone worked together to build benches of fallen timber. There was something satisfying in changing the place, in adding to it so that it became less a place of loss.

Some things never changed though. Danny, afterwards, with his guitar blowing in the wind, sitting on the hearth back at home, strumming, strumming, and always cold. Every year at the mountain he wore another layer of clothing. Something going down with his thyroid, Karen said. And Patti wore the same vest every year – brocade and denim – though now, more than a decade later, she was armed and designed with a fair supply of business suits. More often than not, she and Danny slept together that night, and Jon and Karen saw them for breakfast the next morning. To conjure memory, things people did. It was tough when you loved someone and they were gone. Jon had a half-notion that Patti was just a little in love with Murray – maybe more so now.

Elsa and Peter called Jon Dad; Murray was Father. They had five grandparents. 'I'll be the spare,' Jon's father always said, and his mother would kick his shin. 'You're not a tire, Burt,' she'd say.

And they weren't a camping family. The few pieces that Jon and Karen did own had been collected for the November day, though they did use the one-burner propane stove for the odd day they spent on the motorbike. In November, the stove was used for coffee or hot cocoa, along with the dozen or so enamelware mugs. There were ponchos for rain, in red and yellow. The day before, they always checked everything; the next morning, they packed it in the back of the truck.

Jon's Cowichan sweater hung by the door. He pulled it on, and his scarf – first Christmas gift from Karen – worn enough to have a hole in one corner. She'd say something about buying a new one, but Jon was attached to the gift. Karen was always buying new things. She wasn't frivolous, though; she replaced worn-out things. Jon would never have remembered to renew his toothbrush. She did: usually green, every two months.

Jon let himself out of the basement. For a moment there was silence. He couldn't hear a voice from the kitchen. The packing must have been finished. All was silent.

That wasn't how he wanted it. He stood waiting until he heard a noise: a door slam, a shout from Peter. Elsa's abrupt return. The voices of his children. Then he could turn and leave.

He walked the back road – not the main with its sidewalk and blasting cars. The back way, as they called it, wound down a side street, cut through the driveway of a townhouse complex, another short street, a fenced walkway which opened to the back of the library and a small-town cluster of stores. And the pub – Murray's pub. They had all spent time there, the men more often, after work and for playoff games.

In the old days, Danny'd played acoustic there. Not for cash – he didn't play well. He played for his friends and for a pint. But no one played at the pub any more. Jon suspected it might have something to do with Murray, though the years had passed, and the patrons had aged and many had moved away. Perhaps Murray was the reason for the strange sobriety of the place, though time had blurred the reason, and many of the people who passed time there thought of it only as a place with music low enough to exchange words, a place where the bartender never had to take away keys.

Jon pushed through the door and sat on one of the stools drilled into the floor by the bar.

And there he was – Murray – just as he might have been that night. Jon would swear it was dark outside the windows suddenly, and no longer late morning.

'Murray,' he said.

Murray nodded. Or his head angled downward. His movement made Jon look away for a moment; he had to remind himself where he was, who he was. There: the bartender was waiting for his request. Their usual ale, as they'd shared before. He slid one in front of Murray. Murray looked at it, his head angle unchanged, ponytail gray as the photos. But no more so, Jon noticed.

He held the glass just under his nose and smelled before putting it to his lips. He emptied it as Jon watched. He had a thirst.

Jon pushed his own glass in front of Murray then, asked the bartender for another.

With the second drink, Murray was like an old woman at her tea. He sipped, sipped again. Held it to the light. There wasn't a line on his face.

The door to the women's room rasped open, squawked shut, distracted Jon for a moment, caused him to think of windows slamming in old wooden frames. He had a sudden image of white cloth fluttering with a gust of wind – curtains, or wings. He shook his head, and turned back. Murray was setting his glass down after a long draught – yet that glass seemed never to empty – and he was rolling the liquid over his tongue, eyes almost closed.

There was the roar of an engine out front of the pub, the squeal of brakes from not far, and Murray's eyes opened. He turned, smiled at Jon, so gently. Jon laughed, but the sound rattled, even in his own ears. He said, only half aloud, 'Murray, we're doing okay, you know.'

Jon held his glass to the light, too, as if he might see whatever it was that Murray had seen in his. *Murray, I can't live up to you.*

He escaped for a piss, and when he returned, Murray was gone. Jon sat with the stool empty beside him, and his fingers traced the pattern that he found in the wood grain of the bar, a map following the path of Karen, Elsa, Peter, the others, up the mountain road, around a knot in the wood. His fingers paused at the knot, a blemish, dark and pocked. He tried to return his thoughts to his home – his mind travelled from one room to the next – but without his family it was an empty place, and he buried his head in his arms like a child at a school desk, so tired. He could feel the eyes of the bartender, and he lifted his head, paid and left, leaving the last glass full – a sort of offering.

The truck was gone of course, but inside the garage was his bike. In the grey light from the doorway he could see it in the gloom, the chrome shining after the end-of-summer polish. The insurance had run out at the end of September when the rains had begun. But Jon's reach for the helmet on the wall was deliberate; he was headstone-sober, exchanging his sneakers for the heavy leather of riding boots.

The bike engine skirled, mistaking the excursion for spring love, and the road rose to meet them. A sign, Jon thought, though his gut curled. He went on, kept the bike steady through the city, around the curve of Lost Lagoon. His cousin had dropped his bike there on a day not unlike this. He bowed lower, clung tighter. The rain had come as he'd crossed the Burrard Street bridge. On the Lion's Gate, it plunged into his face, an acupuncturist, manic attempts to heal. Jon didn't want to slow the bike. He turned north. Would there be snow? Usually if there was, it would be only at the peak. But there could be ice. He went on, past the streets of the city north, to where the houses disappeared and the road narrowed, with cut and naked rock rising to one side and plunging to the other. The rear wheel slipped but held. For a while, at least. Farther up, the wind came fiercer – there were branches in the way – and the road grew ugly. Fear bullied Jon, uppercut fists of wind made him almost call out for help, made him appalled at the size of his need – had he seen it before? The bike slipped sideways and he did cry out then, some word or name he couldn't remember later. He went with it, a downed water skier not letting go. His leg, numb with cold, was suddenly searing. Almost to the edge, and the bike slid from between his legs. Jon was flung away, over the road, across the ice he'd failed to see, stopped on the far side by orange rock. He lay there, listening as the bike ripped through brush, passing minutes until it whined to the bottom of the gully, wondering why he was where he was instead of at the bottom, bones broken, crumpled in the creek. Gravel pressed into his cheek.

He waited for the movement to still. Then wondered if he was dead. Injured. Alive.

He moved, tested joints and parts. Stood, like a baby calf. Trembled and sat again, but found his mind moving still along the path of wood grain. Karen. The children. It wasn't far to where they were. He could walk.

He slowed his breathing. The bike was silent finally. The place was silent, though Jon listened for some sound. Nothing. He was alone.

The hike took about half an hour. He stopped twice, once dizzy, but he got there, could see Danny pouring boiling water from the stove into the coffee pot. Jon knew then that he was hungry. Though his leg still pained him, he straightened, no longer climbing uphill. Patti he could see, sitting on a bench, Peter with heavy eyes, leaning against her. The ceremony – memory and thought and two minutes – was over.

Elsa, arms around her mother, saw him over her mother's shoulder as she lifted her head. Karen turned. 'Jon.' Her eyes were full, and she stared at the side of his head until he put his hand up to his temple and pulled it down, blood on his fingers.

Then Karen struck him hard, and he was glad. It hurt.

Gingerbread

I REMEMBER waiting on the window seat, watching through the front room window for her to come home from the bakery. The window seat wasn't a warm place at that time of day in the noon of winter, but from there I could hear her steps on the sidewalk, the sound of the latch lifting on the gate, I could see her come up the walk, always in the navy bouclé coat. I'd loved the woollen loops when I was younger, when she'd first found it in the grandmother's closet.

'Just like new,' she said, when she began to wear the coat. 'It's never been worn.'

By then, though – the night I remember – it was very worn, missing a button that my mother never replaced, and the hem pulling away. The door opened. She hadn't raised her head, hadn't seen me in the window, but instead of the long-day welcome I'd hoped to see on her face, there was only an expression of acknowledgement, as if I'd just come in from the next room.

'Bea,' she said.

'I have something for you – in the kitchen.' She followed me down the windowless hall.

'It's so dark,' she began.

I took up the packet of matches I'd left on the table and lit one after several tries.

She caught her breath.

'It's okay,' I said. 'I practised over a sink of water.'

I lighted the candles in the centre of the table – three I'd found in the drawer of tea towels. Keeping warm under dishes turned upside down there were grilled cheese sandwiches cut in corner-to-corner quarters, and two bowls of tomato soup with skin formed over it. Beside the candles I'd set two spoons and a skimpy plateful of grated cheddar, now with curling edges and rising oil.

'I just need to lie down.' Her hand was on the door jamb. 'Then I'll eat. You go ahead, though.'

I turned on the overhead light after she left, and blew out the candles. Wax sprayed over the tablecloth, stretched into tear shapes and hardened quickly in the cold soup.

My cousin Laurie could dance on her toes and leap so high that she flew.

And Peter would be the youngest in his law class. The uncles talked about him. They would leave the firm to him, and to Jennifer, the youngest next to me. Jennifer still played with dolls, but she lined them up along the edge of the bed where they acted as jury and she would pace in front, letting them know why they should believe that her client, the stuffed bear with the missing eye, was innocent.

There was such a number of them. Cousins, all with siblings and schedules. The homes of my aunts and uncles were filled with swimming pools and leather furniture, abstracts painted by local artists, and photograph portraits: Laurie in tutu with the National school; Kurt with his rowing team – the medal hung by the photo frame.

My oldest cousin Mel painted my nails shiny pink, and Peter gave me his old books. Nathan showed me how to tie my shoes, and Elizabeth tried to teach me the facts of life, with drawings on coloured paper.

'Let's give Beat a ride,' Kurt would say, and he'd be on all fours; Laurie would hoist me to his back, and he'd gallop around the room. I'd be passed from one to the other, until we ended as a heap of exhaustion in the middle of the room. Sometimes in their play I would be roughed – a red ear, a knocked shin – and there'd be growly hugs, or pronouncements of 'That doesn't hurt' now. It was fun, and not often enough.

My mother was the oldest of all our parents, and I was the youngest of the grandchildren. She'd had me late in her life; as soon as she could, she told me, and then it was too late for another. 'My cousins are my brothers and sisters,' I said to her once when I was feeling bad, and she tucked her face into a smile, said nothing, patted my hand.

The veins in my mother's hands were a relief map, tracing a path humped with mountains. The hangnails were places of bloody warning, nails unloved. The hands were old. Take my hand, she'd say, but I crossed the street on my own with her just behind. In the winter months, then with gloves on, I would take her hand, but she never seemed to catch on. When I learned to knit, I knitted mittens for her, bright, of many colours. The first time I had my own money to buy a gift, I bought gloves, red and leather. Anything to keep from having to feel the blue knots.

Mel sat at the bar in the basement of Uncle Luke's house, and practised looking grown up. But it was difficult when Jennifer and Peter decided to fight over the television station. Mel slid from the stool and pushed Peter into one end of the chesterfield, and Jennifer into the other. Then she took up the remote, turned off the television and went behind the bar to find a radio station with music. 'I hate you,' said Jennifer, looking at Peter, but Mel's head appeared over the edge as if she thought it was meant for her. She swung herself up over the bar and back to her stool. 'I hate being the oldest,' she said. 'It means taking care of all you brats. I don't see why I should have to do that.'

'Mel – you don't do anything.' Nathan had come from the billiard room and heard her last words. He pretended to line up Peter's head with the cue in his hands. 'Come have a game with me,' he invited, but Mel sulked.

Peter said, 'I will.' Nathan told him to forget it, then changed his mind.

'All right. Let's teach Beat how to pocket a few balls.'

Mel had found Auntie Mariann's cigarettes behind the bar and she was looking for matches.

'Okay, I'll come,' she said.

'No – you look after the last brat.' Nathan moved his head in Jennifer's direction. So today, Jennifer was the brat. We each had our turn.

I liked the feel of Nathan's hand on my shoulder, pulling me toward the adjoining room with the great mahogany and green table, the low hanging light fixture that shadowed the high ceiling, the racks of cues, the balls bright and chunky as toys.

'Come on, Beat,' said Nathan.

Behind me there was a click as Jennifer turned on the TV.

My mother baked gingerbread. It bubbled brown sugar, molasses and ginger on the stove.

'Your grandparents have been married for fifty years,' Mother said. 'We're having a party.'

The grandparents were always in a far corner, behind all my cousins, quiet under the aunts and uncles. They sat in chairs hoping no one would notice, and now we were having a party for them.

'Where?'

'At Auntie Joan's.'

I loved Auntie Joan's house, with fire so warm and carpet so thick I fell asleep and never woke up feeling I'd missed something.

'Does Grandmother talk?'

'She can.'

Sometimes I didn't know why my mother smiled, what her smile said.

'Does she say anything?'

'Not often.' The heavy pot was off the stove, and Mother was turning flour into the dough. It would pull out a lighter brown as she mixed, the bowl held firmly with a thick oven mitt, her other arm moving from its shoulder with the wooden spoon.

'Did Grandmother talk when you were little?'

'When I was little, once in a while. She was tired, you know. There were eight of us.'

I'd heard that before. Of course: three uncles, four aunts, and my mother.

'I wish you had a grandmother.' My mother didn't alter her spoon rhythm as she spoke. Maybe I hadn't heard her correctly.

'I have a grandmother,' I said.

She straightened, stood taller.

'Of course you do.'

That's as close as she ever came to complaining. If she had, it might have been easier to love her when I was younger. Then again, perhaps I would have despised her. It's easy to despise a complainer.

My mother cut the gingerbread pieces twice; first before baking, with an extra quarter inch around, and a second time after. The edges were smooth then, and easy to join. The gingerbread was just right, rich-coloured, firm not hard, fragrant. I didn't see a recipe book, a pattern, a picture. It was inside her head, and it was as if she'd done it so many times before, but I'd never seen a house like that.

After the pieces were cut and cooled, she stored them away in an old tin lined with waxed paper. A Christmas tin with a scene of children with snowballs and skates. The tin sat on the kitchen windowsill for a week – the week before the party – and I would look at it and turn it and imagine each of the children as one of my cousins. There was Mel on skates, Kurt with his cap peeking over the snow fort. There was Elizabeth. That would be me, small beside her. Mother nodded at my stories.

On the fifth day we went to the candy store, and mother let me choose quarter pounds of peppermints and coloured creams and fruity jellies. The man behind the counter explained to her how to melt the bright hard candies, how to make a mould of licorice strips, how to make stained-glass windows, miniature, to fit the house.

There were great bins of cookies, biscuits, wafers. Not like the thick hand-shaped peanut butter cookies at the bakery. These were fine thin cookies, with cut-out letters or dustings of sparkling sugar. 'These for the roof?' mother asked me.

I was not accustomed to questions from my mother. It'll look like frost, I thought to say, but too late. She was having the man weigh them, and he wrapped them in white paper. She handed them to me though, and I carried the packet, with care for the brittle edges.

Before Laurie went to dance school, I saw her. She was wearing a leotard as usual, the colour of the forest, and I found her in the grandmother's bedroom in front of the only full-length mirror in the place.

Laurie's feet amazed me, and her kneecaps: she was always moving in two directions at once. I sat on the bed and watched for a while. She didn't speak, and I admired the set of her mouth, the stretch of her neck, her curving brows. She curtsied at length, and then spoke.

'Do you know the grandmother used to live in that bed?'

I moved to the edge of the red-and-blue quilt.

'Right there.' Laurie pointed to the side I was on.

I stood. 'Right there?'

She nodded. 'The grandmother lived there for years. She never got up, never left the house.'

I thought of the grandmother as she was now, in her chair, quiet. I' d always thought she seemed old and tired, tired after living in a house with eight children. 'How could she have stayed here for years? Did Grandpa cook? Who looked after all of them?'

Laurie shrugged. 'I don't know.'

My mother cut a large square of cardboard from a box with a knife like a saw. Her movements could be too quick to follow. She covered the board with aluminum foil. 'Looks like a smooth sheet of ice, doesn't it,' she said. She handed me an egg and a small bowl. 'I need the white separated from the yolk.'

I'd broken eggs for her before, but never separated. She showed me how, with the two halves of shell, the rim of one half cupping the yolk as the slippery white pulled away. She could be a patient teacher.

'Did it bother you that you had to wait so long to have me?' I asked.

'I dreamed of you before.'

'How did you know I'd be me?'

She touched my head. For once, I didn't pull away from her bare hand. 'I knew.'

My mother never talked to me about my father, but my cousin Nathan did.

'My dad says that your father was the perfect man for Aunt Kate.' (That's what they called Mother: Aunt Kate. The other aunts were Auntie, but Mother was Aunt.)

'My father was a perfect man?'

Nathan nodded. 'Aunt Kate sent him away.'

'She never said that.' I challenged him, but without spirit.

'She did.' He shrugged. 'Right after you were born.'

My mother set the bowl of egg white icing in the fridge. 'We'll let this cool. It'll work better. When I wake up, we'll put the gingerbread pieces together.' She slipped off her house-socks, ugly woollen things. I could hear the wool catch in the backs of her heels, so rough and cracking.

I loved my mother's face when she slept.

When she was awake, when she moved from the sink to the stove, to the fridge, her skin was red, and when she came through the door from the bakery, her face was mottled, her eyes tired. But asleep, she extinguished the thoughts that made her eyebrows gather; perhaps there was even a hint of smile to her lips – I liked to think so. The lines that counted her years fell away, and I could see a likeness there, to my aunts, Joan and Win, the youngest.

Sometimes when my mother slept I would slip the old photo albums from the stack in the bookcase, and turn the pages. That day, the day of the gingerbread house raising, I took my favourite album from the pile – leather-looking, a cord drawn through the holes in the pages and covers, silver corners holding the photos – and noticed for the first time how there were so few pictures of my mother. It came to me, though: she was the photographer. I looked long at the few that were there, one in which she stood behind her mother's chair, so tall and without hips that she reminded me of a porch pillar. The grandmother looked into the camera waiting for the moment to be over. At least, that's how I interpreted the expression on her face: a look of enduring, long and afraid of suffering. The grandmother was not the strong person I'd supposed. I'd looked at the photo before and had never seen it, though. I had known that a photograph could skew a memory. Now I knew that a bit of knowledge could add to a picture another thousand words, and I was ready to believe Laurie.

There was a man in one of the photos, maybe a friend of Uncle Jack's, though he was older. There were no pictures of that same man with my mother, so I had no reason to hold the thought that I did. Still, he turned up a few times, warm-looking, but always slightly apart.

'Where did you send my father to?' I asked as soon as she turned my light out, her hand on the door to leave me for the night. It felt safe, asking in the dark.

In the glow from the hall light, her silhouette bowed. 'I didn't send him away,' she said. 'Good night, Beatrice.' She closed the door.

The car was packed. There was bean salad, and green. Pickles already quartered in the blue glass dish, with waxed paper and foil wrapped around. A gift in gold paper for the grandparents. 'A kettle,' Mother said. 'They've been using a pot to brew tea, hoping it'll last.'

Last until what?

An extra set of clothes for me, to play outdoors, and pyjamas for the evening. I liked to change to night clothes when we were visiting family late; then I could pretend to fall asleep on the way home and Mother could carry me up the stairs to my bed. And even as she muttered about my size and my weight, she'd pull my quilt over me, whisper good night.

'Now for the house,' she said, when the car was packed. 'How do we take the house?'

The back seat was full of the tools she'd borrowed from Uncle Luke for the basement fix-up she'd done in the fall.

'My elbow will catch the house between the front seats,' she said.

Together we returned to the kitchen where the house waited in the middle of the table. It was the most perfect thing.

On each side of the roof there was a dormer window; meringue wafted from the chimney made of red shiny beans set in mortar icing. A gingerbread couple – the woman in lat-ticed white icing, the man in raisin suit-buttons – stood in the garden in front of the house, a sifting of fine sugar snow over their world. A bell hung at the doorway, the door stood open. Chocolate stepping-stones, shutters at the windows, a rustic fence of pretzel sticks, a mailbox of opened truffle on a pep-permint cane, and a tree – a real twig – decorated with birds, each a unique creation of jellies, chocolate, coloured cello-phane. I touched one and it swung on a thread.

'I made those last night,' Mother said.

I felt odd, hearing the pride in her voice. The birds – the house – had taken such time, and her pride was rightful. I didn't begrudge her, but what then? I wanted to take up the house on its silver tray, and carry it to my room, set it on the table beside my bed, where the late afternoon sun would find the stained glass, level so that I could see past the couple, past the open doorway, into the room. I could live there in my thoughts. The fireplace could glow with real flame. My mother could laugh there, a laugh free of years. A laugh such as I'd never heard.

'We can't put it in the trunk,' she said. 'It might fit in that box.' She pointed to the box in the corner behind the door, the box where we kept potatoes and onions. 'We can clean it out, line it with a towel, put it at your feet.'

I picked up the house, surprised at how light it really was. 'I'll hold it on my lap,' I said.

'All the way to Chilliwack?'

I nodded.

Mother didn't argue.

I thought about the questions I could ask my mother. She never really answered questions. Perhaps there was one, the right one, I could ask her. Then there was when I should ask; Chilliwack was almost a two-hour drive. If I asked her while we were still close to home, she might not answer at all; she might be afraid of more questions, digging questions. If I asked as we neared the grandparents' house, I would never get an answer. After an hour – halfway – she might answer. To keep herself awake, perhaps. Maybe if I didn't put it to her as a question.

'Grandmother stayed in bed for years,' I said, looking out my window, the gingerbread house now growing heavy on my lap.

'Who told you that?'

Did the car swerve slightly?

'Laurie.' I jogged the house over my knees.

'She was ill; we thought she was going to die.'

'But she didn't.'

'No. She didn't.' Mother's voice was small. 'After Win was born, your grandmother stayed in her room. She said it was her legs. Sometimes she said it was her heart. Once she told me she couldn't have any more children.'

'Why?' I asked before I thought. If I asked too many, the answers might stop. But she went on.

'I don't know why. I think she might have been afraid.'

'Afraid of what?' But Mother didn't answer that question. She didn't even seem to hear it.

'I took care of them – baby Win and the others – and then one day when your grandmother was older, she climbed out of bed. She said she was all better.'

Usually Mother opened the car window to keep herself awake, but I knew she wasn't at all sleepy; the cold air, filled with winter fog, rushed into the car, and I wrapped my arms around the gingerbread house to protect it.

'I'm sorry,' Mother said, and she wound up the window. 'I'm sorry.'

I wanted the grandmother to see the house. I set it in the

middle of the dining table – the room was still and dark – and went looking for her. For Grandfather, too. But I couldn't find them; they weren't in any of the places I'd expected them to be. And when I came back, it was too late. The dining room lights blazed fully, and Nathan was handing to Peter an angle of gingerbread and sugar wafer that had been dormer only a moment before; Laurie had the head of the gingerbread man between her teeth, though she plucked the buttons from his suit. 'I don't like raisins,' she said.

Jennifer pulled at the tree, held it upside down, and the birds swung wildly. Several fell to the floor. Elizabeth scooped one from where it had fallen. 'Aunt Kate made this?' She pulled the cellophane wings from the body and scrutinized the chocolate-shavings nest before popping it into her mouth.

'Meringue,' said Mel, as she pulled at the candy plume of smoke. Then she broke the chimney from the roof and handed it to me. Her arm stretched long and white from the velvet of her dress, and I remember thinking she was too old for velvet. I shook my head. I didn't want the chimney. I knew how the candy would taste; I did not want to eat it. I didn't want to see the house in pieces: broken bits of gingerbread corners, walls overturned. I didn't want to hear the surprising dried snap of the icing that had held those corners and walls together. I didn't want to hear the exhilarated shouts.

I didn't want to yell amid their sounds – and I couldn't cry. Not then. I kneeled, picked up the raisins from the carpet, closed my fingers over the baked hard bits. I was certain no one noticed me leave. I went to find my mother, to lead her away, to find some corner where I could distract her with a tale of mine. Or ask for one of hers. Or capture her fingers in a string of cat's cradle from my pocket. Anything to keep her from that room.

Learning to Live Indoors

THEY MET ON A CAMPING TRIP — the first time camping for both — with a group of friends. The friends had arranged it, though no one had intended for Audrey and Matthew to fall in love. They were quite unlikely really. Though later, those same friends were heard to comment that they didn't know why they hadn't seen it before: Matthew and Audrey were well-matched. They couldn't remember why they'd thought otherwise.

That was after their first summer, when Matthew unpacked wilderness sports stores, and Audrey read books on survival and edible plants. They both grew adept with a hatchet, turning logs to blaze and shelter. Matthew learned the skill of lighting the smallest conceivable stove — the fold-up, pocket model — and how to fish without a rod. Audrey learned about strawberry-leaf tea for diarrhoea, and fireweed core for emergencies. She learned the difference between the hemlock and ostrich fern: one was poison, the other like asparagus — on toast, a treat.

Audrey didn't meet Matthew's mother until late in the fall, just before winter set in, and after they'd packed away their summer gear. The following spring they were married. The wedding was a sunrise affair, and the wind on the mountain peak was too cold for white lace.

Matthew's mother proclaimed then that he and Audrey had a problem with learning to live indoors.

'Mother doesn't understand the open night sky,' said Matthew.

Audrey wondered if her mother-in-law's talk had more to do with one of her many parlour games, the rules for which she kept in a loose drawer in her head; she knew so many, and didn't at all care for baseball, soccer, even cycling – anything under the sun. Anything with a chance of rain.

Her favourite game Audrey discovered at her own bridal shower: Matthew's mother distributed clothes pegs to her guests, and had them clip the pegs to their garments. Then, when one woman spotted another with crossed body parts, she was to leap up and wrest a peg from that person who had forgotten and had crossed arms or knees. Even those who crossed at the ankles were caught.

Matthew was amazed to hear of it and asked Audrey again to describe the proud row of pegs clipped to his mother's blouse front: pegs she'd plucked with a loud cry from hems and pocket edges and sleeve ends. She won twice, but declined the prizes. She was the hostess, she said, and it wasn't at all right.

'But my mother doesn't like sport and games.'

'She does like games. She likes rules, really,' Audrey observed with more care.

They never did tell his mother about the bottle of Glenlivet they knapsacked up the mountain, how they sat at their fire sipping, taking turns with the foot pump and every one of eighty balloons – red, blue, pink, orange. How they filled their tent with them, *Bon Anniversaire*, on all. It wasn't either of their birthdays, though Audrey pointed out that their fifth anniversary was only six weeks away.

'Besides,' she said, 'We can be like the Mad Hatter and the March Hare.' She wished Matthew a very merry unbirthday, and he asked, 'Who's the dormouse?'

'Your mother,' she said, and they contemplated stuffing the woman into the aluminum kettle.

He lifted his plastic mug. 'To mother.'

Maybe Ezra was conceived that night. Hard to tell; Matthew had talked Audrey into giving up birth control and even calendars long before. When it happened the surprise brought joy. Audrey thought joy was a cliché, but she found herself experiencing a number of clichés and it was not a bad thing.

She succumbed to morning sickness, though she was certain there had to be some way out, just as all the natural childbirth books promised. (She read every one.) But if there was, it was too late to find and she moved on into the thick number of changes that would shift her personal planet one degree at a time until the season was transformed, and the climate one she did not recognize, and she would wonder: how did I get here? Matthew's mother may have feared chaos and liked rules, but Audrey had no natural sense of direction, and feared being lost. She needed maps. She understood maps. She could read their lines and words.

Matthew was dyslexic and had never learned to read words, but his mother said that was because he'd never wanted to. He read stars and clouds, and was like the magnet of a compass.

When Audrey was six months pregnant, they went hiking, the first overnight climb of the year, up Garibaldi. For once Matthew carried the kitchen sink: their name for the pack, the tent, mattress, and food. Audrey carried one sleeping-roll – it was handy to sit on – and the pot and kettle clanked at the side of her small pack. All the winding way up they wielded names.

'Jonathan,' suggested Matthew, and he imagined the hand of a sunny child in his.

Audrey shook her head. 'Joe,' she said. He can be anything, she thought, and felt strong.

At a fork in the trail they decided. 'Ezra.' They weren't much for biblical stuff; they just liked the letters *a* and *z* being in the same word.

'Mum won't like it,' Matthew shook his head.

'I don't suppose she will.' Audrey leaned against a rough stump, high as a stool. 'Oh, well,' she added, and shrugged.

But Matthew was wary of his mother with her straight lines and vacuum cleaner.

'She has an enormous glass jar,' he said once to Audrey. 'She's waiting to pop it over us. And we won't even see it.'

Audrey laughed. 'You do sound worried, Matthew. Believe me, I'll know it if she ever does.'

'You will let me know, won't you?' Matthew asked.

'Of course.' Her promise was an easy one.

'Which way now?' she asked as she pulled herself away from the stump.

'This way.' He reached for her hand. 'Come on. I won't let you get lost.'

Audrey began to collect books on how to care for children: books about the first twelve months, the first five years. Audrey didn't know many children, but she assumed she understood children because people told her she was child-like, and because she had been a child. Maybe too, because her father had left when she was still young, and some part of her – the part that he had known – had never grown up. Was waiting for him to return perhaps. She wasn't sure that she could pick that part of herself clean from the rest and know it, but she suspected that though she wouldn't thank her father for what he had left, she was glad he had. It was a part of herself that she was most careful with. She allowed it to hide behind the coats in the hall closet when she went visiting; she didn't force it into public. Public made it shy, and Audrey had yet to learn what emboldened the little one.

Ezra fell asleep soon after he was born and he slept for hours. Audrey watched him, and when he awoke, he opened his eyes and she held him, and she saw that he knew he was human and that was all he needed to know. He would always be with her.

Matthew never asked Audrey what were the words in all those books about children. His parenting was instinctual, his movements always slow, his voice low, he knew his child's mind. He set off parenting like a child in a rowboat with one oar. He did not pause, but went on, while Audrey followed the shoreline. He knew she had a rope that she could throw to him if he called, but he didn't. There was something fragile and wonderful about being in his simple craft, and Ezra liked to be there with him, it seemed. He laughed whenever Matthew picked him up, and he smiled first in his arms. Matthew believed that Ezra knew what it was to be in open spaces, and to trust.

Ezra seemed to want to fill his first year with many more. He crawled early, and five days later pulled himself up on the furniture and the walls – he'd straightened his legs and walked in the air since birth.

His grandmother couldn't remember what it was to have a child, but she enjoyed folding diapers, and she knitted blue slippers with pointed toes, and a set of curious little pads for his knees. She took to spending two, three evenings of every week at their home, and when Audrey was tired, she would bathe Ezra, snap him into his sleepers, and Ezra would observe her the while. He was watching for something, it seemed, in her boxy face, until one night he found it: she liked to be teased, he discovered, as he splashed her with bath water. She laughed, loudly, for the first time in so long.

Audrey tucked Ezra into his crib, and Matthew drove his mother home, quiet and humbled.

They always kept the bathroom doors closed. As soon as Ezra crawled, it became habit.

Close the door. Is the door closed?

[37]

Ezra was playing with his Christmas spoon set, so innocent. Matthew heard Audrey's cry through the heating vents in the house and later, in his sleep.

They didn't want to remember who had left the door open, why the waste basket had been in front of the toilet, like a step. Remembering would have meant more death.

So they closed some part of their minds, never questioned, promised themselves they would not let go of what they had left.

Matthew's mother expected a funeral. She telephoned her church, her minister appeared at the door suited in grey, she telephoned friends. Audrey watched her – her planning and organizing.

'She knows exactly what to do,' Audrey whispered to Matthew at night. 'How does she know?'

'It's her way of dealing with it,' said Matthew.

'With what?'

'With grief.' He was angry that she should ask.

'She really believes in funerals.'

'She believes in closure,' he answered.

'Closure,' Audrey repeated, like a child learning. 'Closure.'

'Stop muttering. You need sleep.' And Matthew held her fiercely.

Matthew had believed the dead could metamorphose into a tree or – in the death of an older, stable person – a rock: something he might encounter on a climb. But that night, the week after Ezra died, that night he stared up into the well of stars, wondered if he was at the bottom looking up, or at the top looking down, and he listened to the pines and the river.

All those years of believing nothing dies, and then feeling dead nothing. He'd thought only of change, not extinction, and while Audrey finally fell into a sort of sleep, Matthew lay there, waiting to feel. He reached out his arm into the sky, his hand plunged the dark, stars were close, so bright, and he drew his hand back, empty. He'd been the one to suggest the night under the stars. What had he expected?

He didn't move, not to one side or the other, not to look at Audrey. In her sleeping face he might have seen his son's. He didn't move until almost morning.

That night they left the tent at home and drove to a place they knew of, the other side of Hope. A waterfall. But Audrey said it was too loud, and they stayed by the river, listened to the river's pulse and gurgle. *A cord to the mother-belly,* thought Matthew. *The river,* thought Audrey. Audrey had tied the heavy canvas of the old tarpaulin to a branch, angled it to the ground like a lean-to, and weighted it with stones. Matthew chose to sleep at the outer edge, Audrey chose where the canvas would pass over her, would keep the wind away.

Though it was a damp May, they slid their log-fire into the current before they tried to sleep, and it was as if the water could not quench the flame; the wood glowed orange as it disappeared from sight around the bend.

Neither spoke of the cold after the fire.

They lay looking at stars through branches and their breath was not even. Audrey wondered why she'd bothered with the tarp. It moved with her shoulder and smelled musty. She turned to look at Matthew beside her, lying on his back, his hands to his chest. His eyes were wide open, and as she watched he opened his mouth, took in night air, and a shudder passed through him. She put her hand on his arm.

Audrey fell asleep, if only to escape, and when she did awake, Matthew had not moved.

'I'll sleep on your other side.' She touched his shoulder gently. He didn't move. She didn't want to be under the tarp like that. She passed her body over his – was he asleep with his eyes open? – and lay down on cold new ground, the sleeping-bag only half under her. She could feel dirt in her hands as she turned herself up to face the night sky. She breathed, though for her it was a different kind of breathing.

In the morning, Matthew was in her place under the tarp, on his side, his back and ribs tight to the angle of earth and canvas, asleep after his night.

Audrey lay looking at him for a while, like so many other mornings of their life together. She waited for his eyes to open as always. But not that morning. So she crawled out of the sleeping-bag, her body stiff – reminding her of what it would be to be old – and she went for a walk. She walked to the water-fall where they'd planned to stay, and past it, up the unused logging road to where they'd never been. She found a trail and followed it as it wound over the mountain. The sun hid behind heavy clouds as a wind came up, and all at once she realized she didn't know where she was. She stood still, waited to hear Matthew's voice; she'd been gone a long while. He must be awake and wondering, worried. Scared, like she was.

'Matthew!' she called. The mountain on the other side of the valley laughed, echoed. She called again and again, then was still and listened to her own breathing. Her heart was uneven. She put her hand over it to still it.

Rain had come by the time Audrey found her way back to the orange-grey tarp over the branch. It seemed hours later. Under the tarp, Matthew still slept. She sat at his feet, moved a finger over his bare ankle. 'You promised,' she said.

So the glass jar came over them. Audrey could feel the change in the air. She was afraid that if she walked far enough in any one direction, she would bump into it. That was when she began to spend time indoors, in their home that was not familiar to her. She thought she wanted to tell Matthew about the jar – she had promised, too – but then she would be ashamed of her need to be indoors. As it was, her need coincided with his need for walls, and they spent time together, which they thought was a good thing.

Matthew's mother was often at their home then. Matthew needed to know how to plant the new raspberry stalks – he was trying to go on – and Audrey didn't mind how the woman filled space. Or Audrey wanted help with the weaving of ragged old chair seats, and Matthew asked his mother to sit with him while he labelled faded photos of his father.

One Friday night she arrived with two not large suitcases. She said she'd stay a bit longer, a few days this time. But she hung her clothes and put the bedside photo of her dead husband squarely on the dresser in the spare room.

She cooked and bustled and tried to warm the house. She turned and smoothed the conversation at the dinner table, when Matthew and Audrey would have had silences, and she answered the telephone when Matthew had prepared the answering machine for calls. She folded the laundry, put it away in their drawers, when Audrey would have liked to make a nest of the unfolded warmth on the couch, would have fancied sitting in its midst until later, just later.

But Audrey minded none of that. She did mind though, when her clouds burst, and Matthew's mother would round the corner, offer a handkerchief, fabric, folded into a square – where did she keep those things? 'Here,' she'd say, then she'd stand with her hands in front, her head to one side, and put forth a face of such practised sorrow.

Maybe she needed a slap, like a somnambulist, just a gentle slap, to wake her. Or should a sleepwalker be led to bed, blankets tucked round, sounds murmured, nothing said?

Matthew's mother organized the basement and the garage, and suggested they have a garage sale.

'Shall we sell the equipment?' Matthew asked, holding a tent pole that had somehow fallen from its box.

'The books too,' said Audrey, and she put the plant books and the campfire cookbooks in a box.

The night by the river had been their last. They both knew it. They gave away most of Ezra's clothes and some of the toys they'd collected. They never used the upstairs bathroom. Matthew's mother suggested painting it.

And then Audrey found the handprints. Ezra's, on the wall. It was not that she didn't know they were there. It was late spring, almost summer and she'd meant to wash the walls as seasonal cleaning. Some strange ritual she'd understood to be part of living in a house: spring cleaning. It did have its outdoor counterpart. But she was so used to seeing the prints – jam-coloured and shades of minor brown – that she had forgotten they were there. The marks continued across the low window glass; sooty-white. Ezra had loved to look out. Ezra.

She didn't like it when her mind stopped there. She would move on for the most part. Except sometimes, when she'd be caught by a glimpse of him reaching for the red gladioli or watching the black ant cross his blanket. Her mind would take a sharp left from stopping, and she'd be in Eden for just a little time: hear him laugh, his baby gut-gurgle; watch him, and the elm leaves rattling over his buggy where he'd lain, eyes up and moving. Then she'd back away, out of that garden, and hear Matthew's mother's voice from the kitchen.

'Life is like housework: you do it because you like to live in a clean home.'

And Matthew's response, too low to hear.

Audrey realized that she couldn't guess what his words might be, though there'd been a time when she would have known.

One day, Matthew's mother scrubbed the walls.

Audrey left the car in the garage, took the four-by-four – it was still theirs – and drove away, no particular direction.

Matthew struggled to learn to read, though the words slipped to the right and off the page.

Across the Hall

HE'S COMING HOME TODAY. He hasn't been home in four weeks. Twenty-eight days, like some old cycle she's known.

Will he recognize her? She's looked the same all his life. Will he notice the dress? It hangs so, and moves too much when she walks. It used to move with her – now it sweeps around, looking for flesh. And it's drafty – what had her mother said? Don't let your kidneys get chilled – you won't have children. But Lillie's had her children years ago.

It's ridiculous, in November, to be lurking in the kitchen at the back of the house, waiting for the sound of an engine, and wearing a cotton dress with summer flowers on it, woollen longjohns rolled up underneath. Like some child, hers even, on a blustery Hallowe'en past, costumed and ready for rain.

She tastes the soup, chicken broth with rice and soft carrots, and hopes he can eat it. She doesn't want to see the needle mark where the tube has been stuck in his vein. But she does want to see. She wants to touch it, to feel his river run underneath her touch, winding and oxbow, through islands and organs, a counting pulse.

Her arms are cold. She wants her housecoat – her robe, her daughter would say. But if she wears it, she'll look exactly as he left her. He won't notice anything is different. Maybe nothing is. But she'd like it to be.

She straightens as far as her sagging spine allows and faces the five-and-ten mirror over the sink where a window should be. Funny old ideas of how a person is supposed to have something to look at when washing dishes, like those children's posters on the walls of the clinic. Look at the fairies in their pointy caps, as they dance the tree roots. Ignore the needle in elbow, the purple-red filling the tube until the person in white says enough. They don't wear white now, the woman in the mirror says, and her left eye blinks. There's a hole where her right eye should reflect. The painted wall looks through – the curling silver behind the glass is cracked and broken. Lillie moves so she can see both eyes in the patchy glass and they are faded, as she knows they will be, but they're shiny too. She doesn't like it when the iris-blue is cloudy. She feels far away. But today her eyes are so unlike her own that she questions. 'Lillie?' she asks, and taps the glass. 'Lillian Jo? Is that you?' She has stood tall for too long. She curls over the sink, and wonders if life might have been different if there'd been a window there. Or nothing at all. Wallpaper or blank white. But she stops looking in the mirror and curves towards her hands of foam and wedding gift plates. The plates have lost their edges and it's taken almost fifty years to scour those wretched pink roses off. Someone important gave them the set; she can't remember who.

She meant to fix her hair in the mirror but has forgotten. Standing straight, looking up, is so hard. She pats it, over her ears, pushes a pin in. And remembers when she could braid it, when it was brown instead of white, when her arms didn't ache held above her head. Without her kerchief she is naked.

Frieda, the calico, brushes Lillie's legs and shakes her tail up Lillie's skirt. Stretches to scratch her, knowing the old woman's vulnerability. Lillie reaches for the embroidered square in her pocket, to put it on her bare head after all, but Frieda leaves the room, maybe knowing with female sensibility that Lillie needs her support. Lillie pushes the kerchief farther into her pocket and follows the cat out of the kitchen, her knobby hand to the wall.

The nurse has prepared the bathroom, given instructions to the boy to put the handrails here, and here. The door has been removed and a sliding one, without a lock, is in place.

Lillie doesn't like the antiseptic smell. She passes the bed-
rooms, both doors closed, and goes into the front room, with
her chair and his chair. She shoos Frieda off his. The cat is
disgruntled, menopausal, Lillie suspects. 'Get over it,' she
says to the animal, and sits in her chair.

Their chairs face each other as they have for so long. Not
in opposition, but not quite honest, not face to face. That way
they can both look out the window or watch television without much effort or conversation.

There is so much to do, but she wants to sit and think
about it. Make plans, but not plot. Funny, she hadn't put too
much thought into the decision before. Had she even thought
of it as a decision? It seems now to have simply happened, but
of course it hadn't been like that. Something had to be done
or said. Something to result in these two separate beds in separate rooms across the hall from each other. How had she put
it? She tries to recall. When was it? Fourteen years, a
December. There was an excuse, she remembers now. Yes –
after his heart operation. He'd been sleeping in the spare
room. He liked it – he said it was more sunny. The birds came
closer to the window. She liked it too. Hadn't that come out
one day? Quite naturally even. It bothers her that she can't
remember the exact words. What had she said to her partner
of thirty-six years?

At first, for months really, she clung to her side of the bed.
Still thinking 'my side, his side'. And their doors, across the
hall, were always open. They called to each other, like children at camp. They wore a path across the Persian runner in
the corridor, reading each other passages of stories, remembering messages from Gwen and Charlie and the children.
When he snored, or his breath rattled, she closed the door.
Over time her door closed more often. She knew he was there
across the hall. He wasn't a newborn: she didn't have to check
every hour to make certain that his breath still came and

went. She liked to lie across her bed, a leg flung to one side, his side. And she told herself that it was good for him to get used to being alone. That was when she thought she'd go first.

They are comfortable with their faithful abstinence, she thinks now. Not abstinence. Abstinence tells of some restraint. There isn't restraint. Perhaps that's why it perplexes their friends, and bothers their children. Gwen even brought a psychologist to dinner. The fellow talked too much about sex and age. What did he know? What did he know of the journey of marriage – the strange turns and crossroads? What did he know of hormones, female and otherwise, and their wane and wax? What did he know of Lillie's surprise when her passion turned and became something else – something that was not bad. And what could he know of seeing oneself in a mirror day after day, never seeing changes yet feeling them in the centre of one's being, and wanting to shout them out? How could one always look the same and be so changed?

But the psychologist was young, as were Gwen and Charlie, and they worked hard at trying to find a niche for everyone. Of course Lillie knew they would have protested at that. They were not finding a niche. They were renegades, free of old patterns, forging new paths, discovering forgotten ones. That's what they liked to think. And Lillie would let them. She wouldn't tell them it was far more complicated than they could begin to imagine.

But enough.

It bothers her that she can't remember the words she used. She didn't say, 'I don't want to sleep with you any more.' She couldn't have said ... what had she said?

And what to say now, now that she feels differently. Or does she? Is she just a frightened old woman?

She stands up quickly, and falls back as the world spins. For a brief second she hears the calliope, and remembers that first evening together, wooden horses with painted wild eyes of red. The sculptor's knife had carved blowing manes, tails out in the wind, but the machine and the music pushed them forward, even into marriage.

It has been years since she thought about that time. She wore a dress similar to the one she wears now. Her usual flowers. And she sat sidesaddle. He galloped behind, never quite catching up. He gave her a flower later, and tucked it behind her ear.

This time when she stands, she moves slowly to deceive the tide behind her eyes, to keep the waves still. Frieda, lying in the corner, watches with one eye as she crosses the room, back down the corridor, to the two facing rooms. She enters the southern room, his, bright with a grey light, but not sunny. There are no birds this time of year. That might help her plan. Her room is so dark, but she likes to think of it as cozy. She pulls the curtains even wider in the south room. More grey light to show the cracks in the white stained walls. It would make a good plant room, she thinks. Green could fill up the starkness. Or it could be a TV room – it's closer to the kitchen – in the winter it would be warmer than the front room. She sits on her husband's bed and bounces gently. The springs are weaker than what she's used to. Another point in her favour. He's been complaining about not enough support for his back. Not terribly romantic though – 'Sleep with me because your birds are away till spring, and my mattress is harder.' Firmer is probably a better word. She tries both words out, presumably for Frieda's benefit, listening in the next room. It doesn't matter which sounds better: she knows she won't use either. Gwen put a great pot of early poinsettia on her father's nightstand. Lillie picks it up and crosses the hall.

She places it on the table beside her bed, but that doesn't seem right. She's going to need another table. She can't take his, drag it across the hall, and leave a gaping spot in his room.

He'll notice immediately and think she's gone mad. He won't take it as an invitation, but as a rebuff.

She isn't prepared for this frightened old woman she's become. No one has told Lillie about her. She fingers the kerchief in her pocket, wraps it around a swollen knuckle.

There's a table in the front room.

She has to sit down again after moving it. She has to sit down even before she puts the poinsettia on it. At least she doesn't need another lamp. There's a tarnished copper reading light over his side of the bed. She says it: his side of the bed. His side.

The bulb has died. She unscrews it and shakes it as always, to hear the gentle rattle of worn parts. Somewhere in the kitchen is a new bulb. He needs bright light to read. A hundred-watt even. Under the sink there is only a twenty-five-watt – Charlie's girl left it the last time she vacuumed. She doesn't understand that her grandparents' eyesight is unlike hers. She told Lillie some technical story of energy conservation.

Lillie picks up the weak bulb. She remembers where there is a hundred-watt. In the south room, she exchanges bulbs, and carries the stronger one to her room. She leaves both bedside lights on. He'll notice something different. The brighter room will attract him, maybe. She stands in the narrow corridor, her hand holds the door frame of one room, then the other. The south is cold with its bare windows and weak light in all the grey. Her room is … cozy. Red with flowers. She hung the sheets on the line yesterday and the flannel doesn't smell like hospital.

Maybe he's too tired to care. Maybe he won't notice anything: not her dress, not the light, not the bedpan Gwen found for her, not the heating pad lying across the pillow that isn't hers, not the glass of water for his bottom plate. Not the festive blossoms.

Hers are the plans of a fool. She feels dizzy and closes her eyes, leans against the door frame. She needs a glass of water, and moves back to the kitchen, reaches to turn the tap and lets the water run for a minute. She catches sight of herself in the mirror. 'Lillian Jo,' she says, 'I only want to hear him breathe. That's all. Beside me breathing.'

There is the sound of an engine. She starts away from the sink knowing it'll take a while for her to reach the door. He'll need his time too, and Charlie will help him out of the car. She stands behind the front door, and checks her dress one last time, makes certain the woollen longjohns don't show underneath. A dusty silk flower is caught in the edge of the full-length mirror in the hall. She pulls it out and tucks it behind her ear.

Second Week of October

THE DOG was taking his duties seriously, as always, and he barked at the blink of a dying streetlight, barked at the gentle wind playing with the leaves, barked to make up for the friend he'd allowed to the door without warning. Martha heeded his sound and turned on the outdoor lights, gathered up her robe, picked up the baseball bat the children had left in her path, opened the door, and stepped outside. Each time there was only silence. Even the wind stopped playing, to mock her. The dog stood at the open door, tongue hanging out of his mouth, a mouth that smiled slightly and mocked her, too. That smile, slight or even imagined as it may have been, irritated her. She thought she might prefer a burglar to being called to the door so often. But she could make use of these dark hours. Thinking that, she remembered her mother, on her hands and knees, washing the floor, working with a knife at the corners, so late, when she believed no one was around. When she had time.

Martha did return to her half of the bed, but not before she refilled the dog's food dish, emptied the stale water, filled it with fresh cold water, shook out his blanket on the porch. He was like another child, which he shouldn't have been – he was a dog. If only she had a little time. She could catch up with all that needed to be done. Or she could have some moment of release from her responsibilities, some room to move in this small world of house and yard. If the day were longer. Perhaps if the night.

The dog would have to go, she decided.

Her thought was wordless. Words could be so binding, and

if she'd taken the time to put words to it, she probably would not have phoned the SPCA.

They sent a man after her husband had left for work, and the children had gone to school, and as Colin napped. The man put the dog in a van. The dog was happy to go, wagged his ragged feather tail. This was what Martha wanted after all, and the dog had no reason to believe that he wouldn't return.

Martha sat at the kitchen table, in her silent house in her silent yard, poured a bit of brandy into her tea and cried. The dog's smile hadn't seemed so mocking in the light of day, looking at her from the door of the van. She left his water and food dishes. She'd empty them later.

The linoleum was dirty and she was afraid to look at the corners where the floor met the walls, but she made no move to get the mop.

Colin woke from his morning nap just as she began to prepare lunch for the others who would soon be home from school for a brief, hectic forty minutes. She forgot about the dog in the melee of voices, and the children came and went, passing through the front gate, from where the dog greeted them every noon with his panting happy breath, his unclipped nails scraping the concrete outside their door as his feet skirmished in anticipation of a small hand dropped momentarily onto the back of his coat, the brief scratch of short fingers digging into fur, as each child passed through the open door.

After they left for school, Martha sat in their silence. The children hadn't seen that he wasn't there. She didn't need to close her eyes to picture the dog in one of those cages. Perhaps by now the dog realized no one was coming for him. He would begin to look worried.

Her husband always laughed at her when she said such things. He said that the dog was not capable of looking worried, or embarrassed, or of experiencing the range of emotions she assigned to him. Yet there was that distinct look on the dog's face when he furrowed his brow, and laid his head across his forelegs, crossed right over left. It was worry. If his head was laid between his forelegs, the look became one of sadness. She knew. She'd mixed his worm pills into his food, shot antibiotics down his stubborn throat, applied cream to his boils and incisions, clipped his coat when leaves were caught in the wool, driven him to the vet's in the middle of the night. She knew that, too.

Martha bundled the baby into the buggy for their afternoon walk. She wheeled out the front door, turning to close the door behind her and at the same time reaching for the hook to the left, the hook which held the dog's leash. Her hand tightened over the worn leather before she remembered, and her hand snapped back as the metal chain collar swung against the wall. She thought she could hear the dog whine. She was suddenly angry that the children hadn't noticed.

She pushed the buggy, wishing the baby wouldn't sleep so soundly. The walk was a much slower pace without the dog to run behind, and they didn't travel their usual distance.

She passed by the school. Wil and Tali were in classrooms in the front of the building. Perhaps they would chance to look out the window. Teddy's grade one group would be in the library. Some of the blinds were pushed up in that room, she could see.

But the children returned home from their day, and her husband from his, and they had dinner together, the children did their homework, had their baths and went to bed. When the house had fallen asleep, Martha got up, stood in the middle of the kitchen, and knew no one had noticed. An entire day had passed and no one had noticed.

She washed the floor.

She returned to bed. 'He was your dog,' she wanted to say to her sleeping husband.

The following morning she scrubbed the dog's dishes, and put them away in the back of the cupboard. She folded his blanket and placed it on a shelf in the garage. She swept the porch of scattered dog biscuits and loose fur, and wiped the glass door of noseprints. His salivated tennis ball she threw into a corner of the garden.

The children came home for lunch and then returned to school. The family was home for dinner, and later went to bed. She spent an hour, early in the morning, sitting in a chair in the kitchen, warming her icy feet near the open door of the oven, pretending not to see the rudely scrubbed naked floor.

The next day was Saturday.

The children played in the yard and her husband raked leaves. Shortly after ten, Wil came bursting through the door holding a pant leg well above his skinny ankle and out from his body. There was a smeared brownish stain at the knee – the leavings of the dog. Martha had remembered the dishes and the blanket, but had forgotten that.

Her husband was right behind her son. 'That damn dog,' he said. 'Damn shit-dropping animal, where's the shovel anyway?'

Martha couldn't think where the shovel was.

'Well. Where's the shovel?'

'In the garage, I think,' she mumbled.

Wil was still staring at his pant leg.

'Take them off,' Martha told him.

'Damn dog,' he muttered, echoing his father.

Martha could see through the window, where her husband was using the shovel. He began to walk slowly around the yard, head down, scuffling through leaves with his booted feet. He bent down to pick up the rake he'd been using, and continued his search. Martha became aware she was holding her breath.

'Now what do I do?' Wil held his pants at arm's length, his

nose wrinkled, his underwear thin and grey with faded Mickey Mouse pattern.

She took them from him, to the laundry room. Might as well start another load. Any minute now the question would come – 'Where's the dog, Mom? Hey, Mom, where's the dog?'

When the soap was in and hot water had started into the machine, she followed her husband's movements, walking from window to window, watching him do what every week she had done. He never raised his head from his task. Tali meandered behind him, her stubby hands in the palms of a pair of Martha's old garden gloves, the empty fingers flapping from the sides of the bag she was holding.

The cry, when it came, was from Teddy. 'The dog's gone. I can't find him.'

Her husband's answer: 'He must be around somewhere.'

The children let it go at that.

Sunday morning, Martha had been awake for hours. Her husband didn't stir as she opened the bedroom door to listen for the baby, but it seemed the baby had decided to sleep late. As grey light began to outline the window blinds, she could hear movement. That would be Wil, waking his sister as he always did. The two were a team. The baby and Teddy would have to make their own way. Martha heard the familiar thunk of knees dropping on to the window seat in Tali's room.

She rolled over, pulled up the quilt, but their voices, even their words, reached her.

'There're the leaves I raked yesterday.' Wil was so important.

'I raked too,' Tali reminded him. 'And I held the bag.'

There was a pause – Wil must have been thinking.

'There's old Fritz on his bicycle,' he said.

'That's Mr Fritz,' said Tali.

There was silence. Martha felt herself finally drifting.

Then, 'Hey!' That was Wil. 'I wonder where the dog is!'

'He's around somewhere.'

'But I haven't seen him,' Wil insisted. 'I haven't seen him in days.'

Tali said something that Martha couldn't quite hear because there was a sudden scramble down from the seat, and the children passed by her door, down the hall to the glass porch doors.

Martha reached for her robe, found the belt on the floor – one loop missing, the other torn – and she wrapped it around herself, pushed a tissue farther into the pocket, into an unstitched corner.

But she was too late. Tali began to cry even as Wil became angry to cover his own tears. 'Mom!' he yelled. 'Mom! Someone's taken the dog. He's gone....'

He burst through the door, and his father turned in his sleep.

'Mom – the dog's been kidnapped.'

'No, he hasn't.'

'But he's gone.'

Martha pushed Wil gently into the hall, closed the bedroom door, went to the kitchen and slowly measured coffee into the percolator. She didn't speak until the water made bubbling sounds rising up through the glass tube in the centre of the pot.

'The dog isn't lost and he hasn't been kidnapped.' Her voice was very slow and she didn't look at him.

Tali's footsteps came down the hall. She stopped in the doorway as Martha filled a mug with coffee, and poured a bit of white sugar into it.

Martha whispered. 'The dog isn't lost. I know where he is – he's at the SPCA.'

'Well, let's get him.' Wil had tears on his face.

'We can't.' Martha sipped her coffee, put the mug down.

'We can't because I sent him there. I phoned and told them to pick him up. I didn't think you cared.'

They stared.

'He's been gone for three days.' Martha looked directly at them now. 'And you haven't noticed.'

'I noticed. It's just that Dad said he was around somewhere.' Wil was defiant.

'No,' whispered Martha. 'You didn't notice. Teddy noticed.'

'Well, I just didn't say anything.'

'You didn't say anything, and you didn't do anything.' Martha's voice wasn't a whisper any more, but it sounded like she'd swallowed some coffee the wrong way.

Tali's voice was tiny: 'What's the place where he is?'

'It's kinda like an orphanage,' said Wil.

Tali stepped closer to Wil. She pressed into his arm, which he kept tight to his side. They reminded Martha of Tali's first day at school: she was with her brother then, too. Martha had thought she'd not have to worry, so long as they were together.

Wil looked down over his shoulder at his sister. 'It's like an orphanage, except they might kill him. They call it putting-to-sleep. But they never wake up.' Wil had his important voice again. 'Do they, Mum?'

'Who told you all that, Wil?' Martha hated the sharpness of her own voice.

'They don't wake up, right?'

Martha breathed before answering. 'It is like an orphanage; sometimes they're adopted.'

Tali stayed close to her brother.

'You didn't even play with the dog any more,' said Martha. 'You didn't brush his fur, you didn't take him for walks, you didn't fill his water dish. So I sent him away.'

Wil tried to step forward, but Tali had a tight hold of his sleeve.

[57]

'We have to get him back.'

'And we'll do all those things,' Tali spoke up. 'I'll play with him.'

Martha shook her head. 'I don't think they'll give him back. He might be with another family now. He probably is.'

'I'll go find him and get him back.' Wil pushed his chest out.

'Phone them, Mom.' Tali pulled at the belt. 'Phone them and tell them they have to give him back. We love him.'

'But it would have to be different. You would have to do things for him.'

'We will,' said Wil. And Tali echoed, 'We will.'

'It's probably too late. He's probably gone.' She wondered who would adopt a nine-year-old Samoyed-mix-something-or-other. When she'd phoned, she hadn't asked how long they keep animals. People always wanted puppies.

When the children told their father at breakfast, he stared at Martha, and a strange look passed over his face. A look that Martha had never seen, one that she could not describe except to say that bewilderment and hurt were there, although why hurt, she didn't know.

'We have to get him back,' was all he said. Then he swallowed and put eggs in his mouth. 'We have to telephone.' He didn't suggest that he phone the SPCA, though.

Tali seemed to have adopted Wil's voice. 'He might be killed.'

Her father looked at her, then used his fork and knife on his toast. 'Of course not. Don't be silly. We'll get him back.'

Later, preparing for bed, Martha asked, 'What if we can't?'

'We'll have to get another dog, I suppose, for the children. A puppy, perhaps.'

Martha tied the belt of her robe – it was a cold night – and sat up in bed, reading long after her husband had fallen asleep.

Monday, with the children gone to school, and her

husband to work, Martha phoned. She tried not to anticipate the dog being still there. He would be gone and the family would blame her. They'd lost their dog, and they wouldn't understand that she'd lost her friend. Now that she thought of it, she'd sent away the one member of the family who would understand why she'd done what she had. The dog wouldn't look betrayed – maybe puzzled – but he wouldn't say anything. He'd wait for her to explain, and eventually she would, if only because he waited so patiently.

The man at the other end of the phone was very understanding. Once he realized what Martha was calling about, his voice softened like a rotted fruit.

'You see,' he said, 'we have a policy. We know that a great deal of thought goes into the decision to give up a family pet, and quite frankly, we don't trust a reverse decision made over a few days.'

'But the children have promised to spend more time with him. My husband too,' she added.

'I'm happy if your family has decided to pay more attention to the dog, but it was you who phoned in the request. We need a promise from you that this dog will be taken care of. You're responsible.'

'Yes,' Martha muttered.

'Maybe you need to learn to delegate.' The man paused. 'There's night school classes for that, you know.'

Martha wanted to laugh, but the tears were too close now she knew the dog was still alive.

'Are you willing to sign a statement that he will be taken care of for the rest of his life?'

'I am.'

'Think about it, talk about it, phone back tomorrow,' the man said before he hung up.

At dinner Martha told them. 'We have to sign a statement saying we'll take care of the dog.'

'Who has to?' asked her husband.

Martha breathed deeply.

'I have to sign it,' she said.

The fork that had stopped halfway to her husband's mouth, resumed its course. 'Fine then,' he said, with mouth full. 'Phone them tomorrow.'

'I want a statement from all of you,' Martha said quietly. Her own voice reminded her of the man's at the SPCA. 'I want a statement saying that you'll help me. That the children will play with the dog and brush him every day. That you will take him for walks, and drive him to the vet's when he needs to go.'

The family was staring at her again.

'I'll hang the piece of paper on the wall. And Wil, you and your father will be in charge of yard cleanup.' Martha began to cut up her roasted potato.

Wil made a face, and her husband did not look pleased.

'Fine then,' Martha said. 'If you can't sign the statement, neither can I.'

'We'll do it,' said Wil, and her husband nodded, suddenly too polite to speak with his mouth full.

They all signed the paper she prepared the next morning, even Teddy, meticulously, with an oversized 'T' and one backwards 'd' – Tebdy. Her husband signed it perfunctorily, with a quick glance at Martha as he laid the pen on the table.

As he headed toward the door, pulling his coat on, he stopped. 'When do you think we can pick him up?'

'I don't know,' Martha answered, taken aback by his sudden childlike manner. 'I'm not even sure that he's ours to have.'

Her husband put his hand on the doorknob and turned it but remained standing as if to speak, then quickly opened the door and left.

Martha phoned the SPCA that afternoon, and after the dinner

dishes were washed up, the family climbed into the car – Wil and Martha's husband in front with Tali between; Martha with the baby and Teddy, in back.

The children tuned their vocal instruments until they caught sight of the building. (Wil read out the letters – SPCA.) And they burst into loud music with all their own wandering parts. Martha's husband held his hands to his ears as they sat for a moment in the parking lot. But he was not angry. He took his hands away, waved them as if he was a conductor, and ushered them out.

Martha followed, Colin in her arms, his face in her neck. The building was very brown, she thought, and she wondered: what had she asked of this place?

Teddy remembered to hold the door for her; usually Tali did, but she was ahead with her older brother. The door swung open and Martha moved forward.

The dog's claws skittered on the bare floor – they hadn't clipped his claws – she would have to, soon. The children wouldn't be able to, and her husband didn't know how.

The dog, who no doubt thought the family had gone on vacation and returned, was happy as a puppy. He barked, almost howled, and brought his forelegs up to the children's chests, as if he wanted to dance. When Martha entered the room he moved even more quickly, his backend not going in the same direction as his front, jackknifing from one side to the other, snapping at the air and tossing his head, so happy to see her. But he was held away from Martha by Tali, straddling him as if to ride, and by Wil, on the floor, his arms around the dog's heavy ruff. Teddy skipped around behind reaching for the curled tail.

Martha fell back even as she heard her husband speaking to the man standing behind the desk. As she watched, the man pushed a piece of paper to her husband.

Through the din of children and dog, Martha could see his

mouth move, eyebrows rising momentarily, quizzically. The man at the desk glanced at her and shrugged his shoulders as if to say, 'It doesn't matter,' and held out a pen. Martha watched as her husband held the paper, signed it, and handed it back to the man, who caught Martha's eye. He waved and mouthed the words, 'Take care.' Or at least that's what Martha thought he said.

Days passed and Martha told herself that all was as before. It was for the best; she told herself that, too.

Except she noticed when the dog crossed his forelegs: left over right. Had it been that way before? And sometimes – oh, not often – his tail fell so strangely. Once she looked into his eyes and didn't recognize him at all.

She mentioned it to Tali, but her daughter looked at her oddly, and she did not mention it again.

Louis and Me and God and Everyone Else

FIRST THING, I turned off the car and opened the garage door, though it was too late and I knew it.

I didn't want to look at him, but when I did, he was in his suit. His Sunday suit, with a Bible on the seat beside him. I couldn't believe he had been on his way to church. But I didn't want to believe otherwise, and there was the rosebush with its roots in burlap, just outside the front door. Surely he'd meant to plant that.

I rarely saw him in a suit, except at Fran's and my wedding and the Remembrance Day parade. Every Sunday morning Louis and me tended the Memorial and those damned roses and that was as close as either of us got to the church ritual. We wore trousers when we were younger, shorts in the summer, even jeans in these last years.

There was only us for so long, cutting the grass, clipping the edges, pruning the rose bushes every fall. All of them rose bushes left by somebody's widow or mother or sister. Fran planted a sunset-coloured one for Kenny, 'cause he had nobody, and Freddy's mun planted his in '48, when she could finally force her phlebitic ankles to come to the only place that marked his death and life.

The rose bushes were old and Louis and me were pretty much used to those thick, spotted, woody branches that spent the winter looking like sticks and always surprised us late every spring with buds that somehow managed to become blooms. But the people who bought new pink townhouses across the street wanted them dug up. At town meetings – or at least at the one Louis and me made it to – these people never said what they'd replace the roses with. Probably boxwood. Something stiff, and green through winter. The meeting was loud and rude and I wondered if any of them ever tripped across the street to read our names on the concrete pillar.

I did speak up, but not very loud. Muttered something about olive branches, but no one seemed to hear.

Louis looked at me though, with those wide eyes that haven't faded as much as mine have. Those wide eyes that made me remember him as he was at fifteen, and maybe it's a funny thing to say, but I don't think he's changed much since then. I know I've changed, but I don't know about him. Sometimes I see him as a fifteen-year-old man with two heavy sacks weighing on his shoulders: one sack full of the war stuff and everything else, and the other sack – I'm not sure what's in it, but it seems to balance the first sack. Maybe Louis himself isn't even sure what's in it. He's just carried them around for so long, and they grow heavier, and for almost fifty years now I've imagined him as this hobo who won't stop for rest and open his pack.

Church is the easiest, I've always thought, and the church I was familiar with was the Catholic one. I've always thought confession was a good thing: like a bath, and stepping out on Monday morning with a pure soul like a new suit, and no cooked cereal on your tie.

But then I remember once, going with my mother, and seeing old Joe Schellenburg burst through the door of the confessional. I remember that because usually the men and ladies and the young people looked so solemn on their way out, careful not to betray the sudden lightness of their hearts, I thought. But there was Joe Schellenburg, miserable and slamming.

Mum quit the Catholic church – I think she was tired when my fifth brother was born – and I never went again.

I'd have to say that I learned to forgive myself. I'd had to, after the war.

All their names are in rows on the concrete four-sided pillar. Stanley Irwin, Fred A. Haro, Kenneth Moss, Edward MacGregor, and the rest. That'd be Stan, Freddy, Kenny, and Ted. Kenny was the redhead. We could always pick him out in camp, in the field, when he forgot his helmet, which he did that day. I found him too. Must've been instant. Lucky cuss, said Louis then.

When we work at the Memorial I think mostly of the army men. Maybe it's on account of working with the ground, the roses and such, and I remember being close to the dirt a lot, Louis and me.

That's Loo-is, not Loo-ee. Before the conscription thing he'd always been Loo-ee – his mother was Québecois and damned proud of it. After, he was Loo-is. Broke his mum's heart, though it was already so cracked it wouldn't have taken much at that point. Louis said being French didn't make any sense anyway. He spoke hardly a word of real French, and never had, didn't even have a French surname, and he should have been Louis anyway. But I'd heard him rattling with his *maman* in something that didn't sound like my mother tongue.

I know he loved his ma. He'd never have meant to break her heart.

Maybe it was all on account of his being big. Louis was always big. I remember him, a toddler, tripping down the broken sidewalk, and he was big then. People used to ask him why he wasn't in school. He had his first job at nine, and played every sport there was at high school. Didn't have any skill, but in a goal he blocked near everything. So it was easy getting him joined up at fifteen. Me on my eighteenth birthday, drunk, hollering my way from the recruiting office. I was a man now – long trousers, beer, and then my papers to be shipped out. And

I was terrified of my girl wanting to get us married. Louis was drunk too, and we hollered him back into that office. Maybe we wanted a little company. Maybe there wasn't a we. Maybe it was just me, hollering, arm around Louis. Maybe I felt safe next to his big shape. He was so proud.

My ma'll be pleased, he kept saying. She thinks I'm just a kid or something.

His ma was not pleased, but I thought she'd get over it, and Louis thought so too.

He was fine till we were on that boat crossing the Atlantic, and then I found him one night, on the deck, hanging onto the rail.

I'm not on the field yet and I've done my first killing, he said, looking at the black water – black, though the surface looked like silver ice under the full moon.

I didn't like the way he was looking.

What are you talking about? I said.

My ma, he said. I've killed my ma.

He put his head in his hands, elbows on the railing. His eyes were still open, seeing through his fingers, to that water. I could see them – his dark eyes – shining from between his fingers.

I'd never heard anybody talking like that before and I wanted him to close it.

You haven't killed anybody, Louis. Your ma, she'll be fine.

No, he muttered, and shook his head. No.

That was it. He never spoke about killing his ma again.

We did what we had to over there, and even though Louis and me have spent every Sunday fooling with them roses and mowing and raking and sometimes just sitting on the bench smoking, we don't talk about that time.

A few of those townhouse people used to cross the street and talk to us. That is, till Louis opened his mouth.

One woman came, with her hands cupped 'round a coffee mug that had *decafe* written across it. Like the others, she talked about the weather – they always started with that – and at least it wasn't about rain. They never came out in the rain. The next topic would be the trees across the street that dripped sap on their cars, then about the dogs that made them afraid to walk. Defecation, one called it, in Our Own Park.

Then they'd talk about the roses. They were always working their way to that.

These scrubby old bushes, the decafe woman called them.

The way she said it, it made me look at those roses again, as if after all these years I might have missed something. I didn't see scrubby old bushes.

If the roses had proper fancy names – and I suppose they did – we didn't know them. They'd always been Kenny's or Teddy's – and I could see Fran's wide hands in the earth – or I'd thought Stan's, or Ralph Cole's. Ralph's roses had been planted by his twin sister, and they were big and yellow and the plant sprawled out every year as if it was trying to get away. Louis always clipped it back to nothing in the fall, but every summer it laughed at us again, just as Ralph had back in grade nine, which was as far as he'd gotten in school. Ha ha ha! from the back of the class. He had a big, yellow sense of humour that guy, and his sister must've too.

I didn't say anything to that woman. I just scrooched down to take a closer look at the bug-holes on a leaf. But Louis. His back uncurled as if he wasn't afraid of his height for once, as if he'd put down those sacks from his shoulders.

He came alive.

When I was overseas I learned things I hadn't thought possible. I learned my God had other faces, and some of them I wanted to scratch. I learned schoolchildren could kill. I knew I could have thoughts that nobody'd want to see, but I learned that nobody had to, and I knew I could look at them thoughts, and while they didn't amuse me or entertain me, I could play with them.

Frances and I were married when I got back home. We'd gone together since high school, and we were married for thirty-eight years before she died. On June 12, 1983. And I know Louis was with her once, but that was before, a long time ago.

I think one time he was going to tell me, but he didn't. We were at the bar and he was soused. He opened his mouth and he paused completely – that is, he stopped breathing – then I said something about the waitress. Just to let him believe I was capable of the same, though I never was. I was Fran's. He must have known that. He must have known I'd forgiven him. I knew it was nothing. Didn't he? She did. She never did say she was sorry. She did say she didn't want to hurt me. But it wasn't me, I told her. It was the boy who'd left this country on a boat. That was who she'd hurt, if any. Not me. And she must've known he wouldn't be back.

It was after Louis came home, and before I did. There was that four months. Seemed I was one of the last shipped out. For a while they didn't know where I was. If I was.

Fran said Louis did it because he needed to know he was alive. She did because she needed to know I was. I held her all night and we never talked about it again.

Louis had been working with the pitchfork that morning, loosening the earth around the roses, and when he came alive, he thrust the fork high in the air. But he plunged it into the ground right in front of him and then he curled his long body over the handle, leaning close to this woman, and she stepped back.

You know who those scrubby old bushes belong to ... he glanced at the mug ... Mrs Decafe?

Why the town, of course, she said as she took another half step back.

He turned and spat on the ground, and I peered at him from under my cap. I didn't want to turn my head and see that woman's face. I watched Louis's.

Those scrubby old bushes belong to them.

He jerked his head in the direction of the concrete pillar as he spoke, then looked over at the roses, and at me. He said, Only two more bushes for this place, then we're all here.

I turned back to the bug-holes I'd been looking at. I didn't like the way he was talking.

The woman didn't seem to understand what Louis was saying.

She said, I think the municipality ought to renew these. My husband's on council. I'll speak to him.

She turned, her coffee mug dangling from a finger and spraying a quarter circle. Drops splattered over Louis like dark rain. He didn't seem to notice.

You can't renew them, he said to her back.

He took two steps toward her, and then I stood and reached for his arm.

Can't renew, he muttered as her loose summer shoes clattered across the street.

What Louis had to do in the war wasn't anything different from anything I had to do. Not that I know of anyway. Hell, we all had our secrets then, though I suspected they were pretty much the same as the next guy's. But they were secrets, or at least things we didn't talk about, so there was no way of knowing if they were the same. Or horribly different.

One day – the fall of '43, I think – I remember something about a woman and her child, and Louis finding them. Seemed there was something else to that story, though I'm not sure I can recall exactly what. Sometimes I have the feeling that there are many things I don't remember. Maybe that's for the best. I do remember the woman clutching at Louis, talking at him in French, while he tried to find someone to help her with arrangements for transportation to a DP camp. After that, he didn't talk with the people in the towns. He kept silent, and would watch my face as I spoke with the balding grandfathers and the pretty women.

I do remember that day, after that woman and her child left. Louis came bursting through the tent door, miserable, his lips tight. His face reminded me of someone long ago.

Sometimes when I used to go 'round to pick up Lou at his ma's, she'd be shaking her head.

Louis, Louis, she'd say, He has the nightmare dreams again, you talk to him, talk to him.

I would nod, but we never talked. What would I have said? Why didn't she talk to him, the old woman? Maybe he'd speak his rough French.

But she never did when she was alive and then she was gone, and then Fran went too. Everyone was dead. Stan and Kenny and Freddy and Ted. And the others. It was just Louis and me.

Town council set a date for the replacement of the roses. They didn't say what they were going to replace them with. Someone – a young-sounding lady – from the municipal hall called me and left a message on my son's machine upstairs.

I told Louis about the telephone call the next Sunday. It was June then and the blooms looked good to us, sitting on the bench.

Maybe if I used more of that insecticide stuff, he said, and he flicked his cigarette ash to the ground.

Maybe they wouldn't look so mealy and people would like 'em more.

He took a long drag and exhaled.

But then they wouldn't smell so good, would they? It's worth a few holes and spots. I thought, he added.

Louis pinched the ember from his half-smoked cigarette, twisted the end, and tucked it into his breast pocket.

They won't be taking them out till fall, I told him as he stood. After the last blooms.

He interrupted. Maybe I should learn how to prune them properly.... Remember once I was going to take that class....

In the seventies? I said. When Fran was alive. She found the ad for the class in the paper. When you came for supper.

Yeah. Fran.

He looked at me for a long moment. I looked at him, then away. I could tell by the sound of his air intake that he'd opened his mouth to say something. But he didn't.

And I didn't. I never said a word. Not one that would have counted for something. Something that would make some change to the bends in his path. Something to ease. That has been my mistake.

It was the young-sounding voice again, on the telephone.

Mr Richards? Hello? When were you last at the Memorial?

Sunday, I replied. Of course. Me and Louis. We're there every Sunday.

Yes. Well. I'm afraid there's been some vandalism. The police would like to meet you there – at half past one. If possible.

She waited for my voice.

I'll be there.

They'd like you to identify what's missing.

I was there. Walked up from the south side where the children's playground equipment blocks the sight of that pillar, till the last minute.

The roses. The damned roses. There were gaping holes in the ground.

[71]

I looked across the street and saw some movement in the blinds of Mrs Decafe's French doors. Then they were still, hiding her.

Who had done this? Kids? They'd be random. Whoever had tortured our roses had left the other plants – evergreens – alone. And hadn't touched the pillar. Hadn't thought to empty the full garbage can.

I walked the semi-circle and named the holes. Stanley, Kenny, Teddy, Freddy, Ralph ...

The policewoman began to carefully copy my words into her notebook, but she stopped after the first.

They're all gone, I said, and I left, walking towards Louis's house, out along the dike to the end, near the farms. The wind pulled at my hair, lifted it, tickled the shiny places of my scalp, laughed at my hairlessness, and I remembered another wind off other water, not a salty river like this. I remembered a time in my life when to destroy was to save. No salvation without destruction.

Louis had always lived in his mother's house, and the first thing I saw was the new rose bush in the burlap sack, outside the front door, a sales tag waving from a stubby branch. The door was open, and I almost expected to be met by the smells of ham and pea soup, fresh bread, cut green onions in a chipped jam glass on the table.

The front door led directly into the living room and there I was stopped.

Autumn rose heads drooped as their roots dried and reached for the dirt that soiled a path to where they were left on the few chairs, the chesterfield, the cracking-finish tables.

That was when I realized that from somewhere behind the house, from the garage, I could hear the weak rattle of Louis's car engine.

.

Cutting

GEOFF AND RYAN were new, always new. They came from back east; that's all Ryan ever said. People – women – never cared where they were from, really. Women wanted to take Ryan into their houses. They didn't want to know who had left him in the basket on the step. He would be all theirs, and he would never leave.

He always did though, and he took Geoff, his son, with him.

They would move on to the next place. And Ryan would talk: about freedom, about never saying sorry, about letting go. 'You never know if something is yours, until you let it go.'

Geoff thought he should try to remember Ryan's words. Ryan had never given him many words. A year before, at fifteen, Geoff had left high school, but he hung on to the bound notebook that Miss Lindsay had given him. He filled it with his thoughts as if his head couldn't possibly be enough for them, and he kept it in his knapsack. His knapsack he'd had since he was eight. There'd been too many schools in his life, too many teachers. Miss Lindsay was the last, and the first he'd remember.

'What are you writing in there?' Ryan asked, peering over his shoulder, breathing smoke from the stop in Moose Jaw.

Geoff closed the book.

Ryan was good with other people's money: he was a salesman and a gambler, and hellishly attractive. He found the hair salon and Fred after one walk through the first mall they came to. 'He has room for us. Sit here.' And Geoff sat on the mall bench next to the planter growing cigarette butts, and waited while Ryan met Fred the owner, and convinced him that he could do something with the back room that had been empty for six years: a fitness club, with weights and bicycles and scales and shelves and shelves of high-priced diet supplements and replacements.

'Ha!' said Fred. He liked the idea.

Ryan and Geoff rented a hotel room nearby.

In the staff room there was always Corinne, eighteen and pregnant. She'd worked the shampoo basins since she was fourteen. And Jackie, with all the efficiency of a high-school graduate. She would own her own salon someday, she let everyone know.

Carla came in often on Friday nights, always on Saturdays, and passed time in the staff room, quarrelled with her mother, watched scissors move. One Saturday, she said she'd come to work. Two girls had not shown up for work the day before. They'd probably quit; that's how it went.

First, Sonya argued with Carla, and from the staff room their voices were loud. At least, Sonya's was. 'I knew having you here every Saturday would come to this. I want you to go home.'

But Carla wouldn't go.

Sonya stood in the doorway of the staff room, her hands grasping both sides of the doorframe, as if she were a gate and would not allow Carla to pass. 'I want you to go home.'

Fred stepped up behind her then. 'Sonya,' he said. 'We can all hear you. And we're two girls short today. Carla knows how to shampoo.'

'See?' said Carla, and she slipped under her mother's arm.

Sonya turned on Fred. 'No way's my daughter going to become a dropout, varicose-cursed, broken-backed hairdresser!'

Fred laughed. 'Ha!'

Sonya lifted her hand as if to strike him, but he moved his short, thick body away. He was good at that.

Short two girls: on a Saturday, that meant four hands and felt like six. Sonya gave up to grim silence, and Carla greeted clients and led them to the basins.

'Come here,' Corinne said to Geoff. 'Watch.' She showed him how to shampoo then; how to cup his hand around the ear, the nape – as she called it – and the hairline. 'Massage like so. Rinse. Condition, especially the ends. Rinse.' She was too quick. Her seven-month belly was incidental. But Geoff was quick, too, and followed every move. It was the first thing he'd been taught that could earn money.

And he was good. Carla grinned at him as they rubbed circles into clients' scalps. She'd learned when she was a kid, practised on her mother and her mother's clients. Perhaps Sonya should never have taught her; why teach a skill and expect a child not to use it.

Carla was born the day before Geoff was. It was an odd thought, to think of her as an almost-twin, but her hair colour, so close to Geoff's, made it easier. Though hers was thick and ripple-curled like a woman's in an ancient painting.

Sonya could have been Geoff's mother, with her Italian eyes, her wiry grey hair, at one time the colour of her daughter's, the colour of Geoff's mother's.

Or perhaps it was the cross clinging to her neck that made Geoff liken the two women. There was something so familiar about it: the heaviness and the tired glint of worn diamond chips. He could remember such a cross from when he was young, swinging over him as he lay to sleep, and scratching his nose. He remembered the whiteness at his mother's throat, and a scent as she put her lips to his forehead.

It must have been his mother he remembered. He must have been very young.

But it was old memory. Now there was Sonya, with her greying hair, so-fine lines running from her top lip, deep laugh lines like parentheses around her mouth. She could have been Geoff's mother, except his mother hadn't lived.

He preserved her memory with care, though, and allowed her to age.

Corinne saw Geoff shampooing and bellowed, 'Fine job, Geoff. You might as well do something while that dad of yours hangs around here.' She didn't like Ryan. She seemed to know without being told that for Ryan there were always backrooms to be had and businesses to be ventured. She seemed to know that he carried his life in a bundle on the end of a stick, and his soul he'd left behind. She didn't like him, Geoff could tell.

Fred did, though. Ryan brought money into the shop, and women: women who poked their noses through the back door and asked if anyone had time to trim their hair. Fred fitted them in with somebody. Corinne began to do more cuts and it was good to keep Corinne happy. She never did thank Ryan. She seemed to believe what fell her way was hers.

She did ask Ryan once why he wore such soft shoes. 'I can't hear you coming and going. You scare the baby outta me, the way you sneak up behind.'

'Has he always worn those?' she asked Geoff.

Sonya ignored Ryan. She was so busy she ignored everyone. When she wasn't cutting hair, she was sketching styled heads on bits of paper: curious little renderings, often not complimentary, but her clients must not have had a problem with her honesty. Even in the brief weeks since Ryan and Geoff had come, there'd been a full cycle of Sonya's clients returning to her. The sketches would be blown into and caught in the corner of her work station, they'd be like a pile of leaves, rustling until Carla came along and gathered them into the garbage. Or they'd be trapped in the spikes of a brush or crumpled in the perm tray. None of her clients ever dared bring magazine photos.

Late Friday afternoon Sonya sat on the one chair in the staff room, her knees crossed, one leg wrapped in an odd fashion around the other – she was so thin – and her pencil prodded and flicked at the paper. She made Geoff think of how he'd imagined a student of art: the way Sonya studied a head, a line here, a bit of bone, contour. Then, again at her paper, her brow furrowed.

It was the grey in her hair that reminded Geoff she was not an art student; she was Sonya, hairdresser, old enough to be his mother, raging mother to Carla. And there was the lab coat. Sonya was of the old school, and she wore a lab coat, with a row of silver alligator-mouth hairclips across a pocket. In the other pocket, though, there were two or three charcoal pencils, and on the outside of that pocket, at the seam, there was the sooty rub of pencil ends.

'Your drawing,' Geoff said. 'Where did you learn?'

She didn't tell him where; she told him when. 'The summer before Carla was born. I drew in the park and people paid for my drawings.' Her voice was not regretful, but still rather wistful.

'You like to draw?'

'Yes.'

'Do you draw anything else?'

'No. Not now.'

Geoff didn't ask what 'now' meant.

'You're doing well with your shampooing.' She changed the subject and commended Geoff. With the side of her thumb, she blurred the hairline in her sketch, and she didn't look at him. 'Ever think about being a haircutter?'

Sonya didn't see the shake of Geoff's head.

'It's not a bad thing,' she said. She breathed out loudly as if she'd been holding her air.

So it was all right for Geoff, but what of Carla?

Corinne came into the staff room, stood in the open doorway. Sonya reached out, put her hands over Corinne's belly. She stared at the expanse of denim jumper. 'He does move a lot, doesn't he?'

Corinne shrugged. 'What's a lot? He's my first, remember.'

'Are you eating well?'

'I do what I have to,' said Corinne.

Sonya untwisted her legs. 'Sit, Corinne.' She stood and was gone.

Corinne sat, took a swallow of the cold coffee Sonya had left behind, and poked a finger at the oxblood leather wallet beside it.

'Whose is that?' Jackie asked from the doorway. She was rubbing lanolin into the cracks in her hands.

'Must be Sonya's,' Corinne answered.

'It is,' Geoff said. Corinne and Jackie glanced at him as if they'd noticed him for the first time.

Corinne murmured. 'I've wondered how old she is. She goes on like such an old woman.'

'Well.' Jackie's joints were like hinges and swung in angles. Ninety degrees, and her hand plucked the oxblood, cracked open the fastening.

'My God.' Her voice was quiet. 'She's thirty-two.' She snapped it closed, dropped it beside Corinne.

'Sonya was sixteen when Carla was born.' Jackie stared at Corinne. They seemed to have forgotten Geoff again. 'No wonder Sonya stares at us and mutters about when she was sixteen.'

'No wonder,' said Corinne, 'she sends the kid to Catholic girls' school.'

They both laughed, and Ryan appeared in the doorway.

'Damn you, soft-shoe man.' Corinne stopped her laugh and bellied past him.

Ryan looked at Geoff. 'What was that about?' His voice was low, and Geoff had to move close to hear his words. 'Well?' He waited with a slow smile.

'They were talking about Sonya. Carla.'

He eased forward. 'Carla? What about Carla?'

It was a small room.

'Sonya was sixteen when Carla was born.' Over his shoulder Geoff could see one of Fred's clients approaching the basins. Everyone else was busy.

'I have a shampoo to do,' said Geoff.

'A shampoo?' Ryan's half-whisper came to him. 'I thought you were going to write. Or was that before you left school?'

Geoff heard his chuckle, the crackle of a match lit, and he smelled a puff of smoke as Ryan disappeared into the back.

Mrs Roland smiled at Geoff. 'They have you at the basins now, do they?'

'Yes, ma'am,' Geoff said.

Her head sank into the moulded sink-front. 'And how's that father of yours doing?'

'Fine.'

'Business going well?'

'Busy enough.'

'Your father is quite the man.' Her eyes closed as the water sprayed from Geoff's thumb. 'If I were younger....' She put her hands under her ribs and laughed, but she'd been suffering from bronchitis and it was not a pleasant sound. 'Anyway,' she concluded.

Geoff wrapped a stained towel around her hairline. 'Do you want a rinse?'

She sat upright. 'Good heavens – I'm not ready for blue hair yet, son!'

'What do you think?' Sonya showed Geoff a sketch of Carla. A three-quarter profile, her face tilted, turned slightly, to show a braid begun near her temple, snaking to her nape, up to her forehead, draped over one eye, and trailing, ending over a shoulder, bare.

For this drawing, she'd taken more time: for Carla's earrings – gold hoops Sonya had bought for her birthday – and for her eyelashes – individual and soft in the shadows that were under Carla's eyes.

'It's for her graduation,' she said.

'That's more than a year off, isn't it?'

'I like to play with ideas.' She held the sketch up to the light. She turned to Geoff. 'Perhaps someday you can go back. To school.'

And be a good boy. Geoff smiled at her. *I am a good boy*, he thought.

'How did your father feel when you left school?' she asked.

'Ryan?' That stopped Geoff. 'I don't know.' It had never occurred to him that Ryan felt anything at all about it. Ryan was a man of action, and he hadn't done anything. Just talked about freedom.

Once Geoff had refused to go home: home was always a boarding house or a one-bedroom apartment, often just a hotel room.

He hadn't really refused though, not like Carla had. He'd said yes as he always did, and then he'd gone to the park, but the park was lonely, and he was home before Ryan was and Ryan never knew he'd been anywhere else.

When Geoff was very young, Ryan had said, 'I'll take you home.' And Ryan would reassure the woman he was with that someone would be there with Geoff when he left his son.

As Geoff grew older, Ryan said, 'You can go home now.' His voice was always muted; no one could hear the wheedling or the force in it. Ryan had never yelled at Geoff. Geoff knew that most people would think that was remarkable.

Geoff had learned that the TV could be friendly, and they usually lived on busy streets where, from the window, he could watch the night or the long afternoon. Ryan was fond of afternoons.

Friday evenings at the shop were long and by the time the last client left, everyone was too tired to go home.

A second wind would blow through the place then and someone would suggest doing someone's hair. Invariably the person chosen would be Sonya. She had the hair of a horse and could take colour after colour. Two days later the colour shed.

'My grey laughs at you,' Sonya said. 'But try again.' And she'd laugh herself.

So Carla took the tint bowl and a brush from the cupboard, and with Alice and Niki suggesting concoctions in a code of letters and numbers, Carla would mix. Geoff stood and watched as she parted the hair, pushed mulberry foam at the roots. Ryan watched too.

Usually he leaned in the doorway. That night, after the oxblood had let its secret, he stood on the other side of Sonya. Though she had her eyes closed, she must have felt his breath on her shoulder. She took no notice, it seemed. And Ryan watched Carla, the slightest smile on his face. *He was quite the man.*

Geoff moved to the doorway, and watched. He could see Carla's face: the quarter that was missing in her mother's drawing, just a pale crescent. She never looked up from her careful colouring, never looked up to Ryan, but now and then her mouth curved with something he said to her. Words no one else could hear. Sonya's eyes stayed closed.

It would have been so easy for Geoff to walk across the

scratched tiles to the staff room, join Corinne there, stand beside her with their backs to the mumbling towel dryer, the vibrations a long-day's massage. He could fold towels into four, his mind with them, neatly, neatly.

But he stayed where he was, though he could see Corinne in the room, head down.

He watched Ryan, his father. Ryan worked until Carla laughed.

Then Sonya looked up; Geoff could see her in the mirror. Just a trace of red at her cheeks, her neck, her convex breast-bone rounded like armour and swelling from her green V-neck.

Ryan met Sonya's eyes in the mirror and everyone could hear his words: 'Carla, you are beautiful like your mother.' For the briefest moment he touched Sonya's shoulder, but she pulled forward, away, and then was gone, heading for the basins and calling over her shoulder.

'The colour won't take anyway. Rinse it out, Carla.' And Carla followed.

Ryan stayed where he was for a moment, his hand still out in mid-air, palm down. He seemed to forget his hand, and he peered into the mirror when he thought no one would notice. Geoff had seen him do that before: stare into his reflection as if he was looking for something.

Ryan followed Sonya and Carla, and Geoff could hear the rumble of his voice at the basins.

Then Geoff joined Corinne in the staff room and folded towels.

'Ever thought about apprenticing?'

'Never thought I'd be a hairdresser.'

'There's worse things,' she said. Her entire belly rolled, but she didn't seem to notice.

There was a noise from the basins. The blend of a laugh Geoff recognized as Ryan's, and a shout from Sonya, which was suddenly cut off as if she'd clapped her hand to her mouth. Her shoes click-clacked to the staff room.

'You're dripping wet,' Corinne observed, and handed Sonya a thin towel.

Sonya threw it down and reached into the warm pile on the dryer for another, which she wrapped tightly around her head.

Carla stood in the doorway. 'Mum,' she said softly – Geoff had never heard her speak like that before – 'Mum, he only wants me there once in a while, when he's really busy. Fred says it's okay.'

Sonya's voice squeezed. 'I'll not have you working in the back room with him.'

'But I'll be working as a receptionist, not as a shampoo girl. That's what you want for me, isn't it? Something else?'

'Something else. Not anything else.' Sonya had picked up the thin towel and was pulling it between her hands. Suddenly she looked at Geoff, realized he was the son of the man she was speaking of. The towel ripped, and she handed the pieces to him.

'Come.' She took Carla's shoulder and drove her through the shop and out. The door to the parking lot slowly closed behind them, and Geoff could feel wind and raindrops.

When Geoff turned to Corinne behind him – for once she was silent – she was standing absolutely still, and her arms were wrapped tightly round her belly.

'Ryan.' Geoff started after him, still at the basins.

He was sitting in a shampoo chair, pulling the green from a fern leaf.

'Why don't we leave this place?' Geoff asked.

'Leave?' He looked up.

'Carla's a day younger than me,' Geoff said. 'She could be my sister.'

He stood up. 'Not if she's a day younger.' His laugh was in

[83]

his throat, and as he walked past, he rubbed the top of Geoff's head.

Tuesday, Fred called to Geoff. 'Shampoo, please.' He trotted to the rear of the shop. When he sat in one of the chairs and leaned back, his feet stuck out. 'A good scrub,' he directed.

But he cut Geoff off halfway through. 'One shampoo's enough,' and he sat up, water splashing down his back. He walked away, sponging his thin hair with a towel, forcing some shape into it. He turned with a grin. 'How's that for an interview, eh? A job's yours if you want it.'

'Mrs Wagner!' he bellowed at his next client. 'Take a seat!'

'Me next, please.' Carla stood in front of Geoff, her fingers picking at a pleat of her skirt. She must have just gotten off the bus after school. Her hair was wet already, but with rain water. The hood on the back of her coat was soaked and pulled away from her neck. Why wouldn't she wear her hood? She stripped her coat off, then her burgundy issue-sweater.

'You've stained your shirt,' Geoff said, noticing the deep red on the shoulders of her white cotton.

'Have I?' She put her head back into the basin and closed her eyes. When clients closed their eyes, they didn't want to talk.

Her scalp was hot under Geoff's fingers, moving through her thick hair, pushing water into it, shielding her forehead, cupping around her ears. She opened her eyes as he tilted her head to catch a corner behind an ear, and he lost control of the hose and sprayed his shirt front. He wished she would close her eyes again.

'Mum's going to do my hair,' she said.

'What's she going to do?'

'Just a trim – the ends are dry. It'll still be long. We've been growing it forever. For my grad.'

'Your mum was working on a sketch.' Geoff wrapped the

towel loosely around Carla's hair, glad her eyes were finally off his face. He led the way to Sonya's seat and pulled a wide-toothed pick through Carla's hair.

Sonya said goodbye to her client, took the pick away from him. She combed Carla's hair back and curly bits escaped her hairline.

Sonya didn't see Ryan as he moved close, closer, plucked the sketch of Carla from her station. Not until she stood and bumped his elbow. He held the paper in his hand and his fingers traced the snake of braid, the bare shoulder.

'Nice.'

Sonya's pale skin was white – whiter than Geoff had ever seen. Her face was so tight and lined, wrung-out. She combed and combed, and finally clipped up most of Carla's hair and bent to snip an inch from the ends.

Geoff heard her swallow then. She loosened the next section of hair, combed it down, stooped again. Carla should have stood; Sonya should have sat on a chair. That was how long hair was done. But she stooped, and missed Ryan, walking away with the sketch.

Or maybe she didn't miss.

With the end of her comb she parted the second section and wound it back into the hair gathered and clipped to Carla's crown. The first section was in its place again, ends trimmed tidy and curls wisping as the hair began to dry.

Sonya snipped across the back of Carla's neck.

There was a sound from Carla. Not even a syllable. More than air intake, though.

Sonya pulled down the next section of Carla's hair and with her fingertips, pushed her head down. That long neck moved forward. The scissors snip-snipped over the guide of the first section. Next section. Next. Sonya drew up Carla's chin with a finger. Carla's eyes were closed tightly. Sonya cut away around her face. Other side, next section, next. All so methodical, schooled. So unlike how she usually cut, when she simply parted the hair, pushed it firmly into place, away, with her comb, while her clips were scattered over her station or still at her pocket edge.

Sonya cut, parted, clipped, cut, and Geoff watched.

Carla's eyes were closed until it was over and Sonya was combing her hair straight back. As the comb left her scalp, Carla opened her eyes. They were dry. A second sound came from her throat. Just an oh. And then she was gone, through the back room – Ryan's room – and out the door. Geoff imagined her through the parking lot, the roadway, out into the fall rain.

Sonya followed Geoff to the staff room. She poured a coffee, but spilled it over the bare toe of her open shoe. She cried out in pain and yanked the shoe off, ran it under the tap, water pouring through the opening in the front. She pulled it over her foot and water dribbled out. There was a rude sucking sound as she stepped forward. 'Damn.' She leaned over – one hand gripped the counter – and removed both shoes. The cross swung heavily from her V-neck, across her face, and she caught it and sent it over her shoulder, where it slithered on its chain to her back. She stood, without shoes, shorter, the chain binding her neck, and the receptionist's voice came hesitantly through the crackly, seldom-used intercom.

'Sonya? Are you there? Your next client is here. Sonya?'

Then a second voice, chirpy and singsong. 'Make me beautiful, Sonya girl!'

That would be Mrs Hunter.

'I'll shampoo her,' Geoff said.

Mrs Hunter was halfway to Sonya's chair, when he met her. 'This way, please.' *I sound like I've been doing it for so long. Like Corinne,* he thought.

He shampooed three times. The second time he pretended to use the wrong shampoo and apologized for having to do it again. Mrs Hunter was beginning to breathe deeply and her head was dropping farther into the basin when Sonya looked around the corner. Her shoes were on.

'That'll do.'

That night, alone, Geoff packed the knapsack he'd had for so long, and he left on a slow bus, on a ferry, to the next city. He knew Ryan wouldn't follow him.

There he found someplace else to shampoo and learn more about cutting.

Family Allowance

IT WAS NEARING the end of the second week of December and Mum was refolding the letter from Donna, my brother's wife. Dad was drinking his milky afternoon tea, and I had mine in my hands, black and hot.

'What are we going to do for a tree?' Mum pushed the pages back into the envelope.

Dad shrugged. 'Patrick's not here.'

'Not this year.' There was a new sadness in Mum.

Dad stood as he did when a conversation had found its natural end. 'I won't be going to the bog then, and there's not a thing in the yard.'

Mum was opening the drawer in the table, ready to slip the envelope there, but she closed the drawer, held the letter over her belly.

Neither of them would think to buy one, and it would be a few years before the tops of the hedge would recover from Dad's cropping.

'What about Marion?' Mum looked at Dad.

Dad looked at me.

'Take Marion,' Mum said again.

He was still standing. 'Marion likes her Christmas trees in pots. Don't you, Marion?'

'I did. Until last year, when bugs climbed out of my little fir and scared the decorations off.'

He chuckled – a deep grown-baby sound. 'You're sure?' Dad asked me. 'You want to cut a tree?'

'It is road allowance, isn't it?'

'Just waiting for us. Just asking for the taking!' He grinned, poured more milk in his mug, cupped it in his hands as if it was warm.

'All right,' I said. Road allowance was land held in reserve. There was no reason for me to feel not quite right about taking a tree. The trees were going to be brought down within the next decade. Someday there'd be another concrete grey ribbon through that soft land.

Asking and taking have always been difficult for me. I've been given so much.

'You can borrow my gumboots,' Mum said, and went to find them, red-racer striped and unused. 'Three years old,' she said, putting them in my hands.

We went to where we'd gone as kids – the bog behind Mrs Sanders' house. Except back then it was Patrick who went with our father to cut the tree. Dad would take me as far as Sanders' and leave me, staring into the silver flash of her artificial tree, always with red decorations and clear lights. Most of the coloured cellophane had long peeled from the bulbs.

As soon as my boots were off, Mrs Sanders pulled flour and sugar and pans from her cupboard, but the shortbread was never done before my father and Patrick returned, and when they returned, it was time to go. Mrs Sanders would let me lick the beaters and scrape the bowl though. There was time for that.

When he was young, my brother carried the tiny handsaw that Mum and Dad had given him. My father would dress in rain gear or work clothes and Patrick was always in his heavy orange raincoat. If it was cold he'd wear long johns and a wool sweater underneath. His orange never changed. Mum must have bought him new raincoats, but they were so like the coat of the year before, and the year before that, that I used to think the coats had simply grown with him. Always three years ahead of me. He had a pair of gumboots too, and I always wanted a pair of those, with rounded, heavy-tooth soles and the red strip around.

I remember one season there was a thick fall of snow, and I spent the entire time at Mrs Sanders' kitchen window waiting for them, wishing I had a scarf like Dad's wrapped round my face, or my toque low like Patrick's, even with his rain hood pulled over. I imagined my short-fingered white hands warm for once in big scruffy mittens.

That year, finding, cutting, hauling the tree, took longer, and the first pan of shortbread was baked.

'Hot rum?' Mrs Sanders asked, standing on the top step outside her glassed-in porch.

Dad shook his head, hardly looked at her as he fastened the trunk lid around the tree.

Mrs Sanders wrapped her arms around and under her bosom, and she didn't speak with a defensive or aggressive manner. 'Marion has to finish her eggnog.'

I stood behind her on the porch, my coat buttoned and my hat in one hand, the glass up-turned in the other, and I drained the slow yellow to the grit of nutmeg, while my brother stood stiff in his orange rubber, and Dad cleaned the saw blade with a towel from the glove box.

It wasn't Dad's way to sit around someone's kitchen. Once in a while, Mum and I would visit Mrs Sanders, but Mum's never been a sociable person either. We're a small-knit family, and close. That is, Dad has always looked to my brother for companionship, and my mum to me, which I suppose is something that would draw harsh criticism from the advocates of Independent Children – those who think aloneness and independence share a house. I think it's quite simple really. My parents like their children, and enjoy their company.

Dad is a quiet man and prefers movement to anything else.

I've never stopped his progression. I've never even spoken loudly enough to cause him to pause. My family has none of the drama, none of that tight-stretching stuff that wastes and pains. Nothing big or sharp.

This year Patrick wasn't home. He was in Sudbury, transferred with his family.

Mrs Sanders' house was still there.

'She isn't still here, is she?'

Dad put his foot to the gas and pulled over the heavy timber bridge that spanned the ditch, as if he thought it might collapse at that moment, and the truck lurched into place in the gravel at the foot of the porch stairs outside the old two-storey farmhouse.

'She is,' he said, 'still here.'

For a moment – second, really – I had the feeling he just might leave me there, waiting at the window, with Lucerne eggnog, beaters, and silver tree. Then the door of the porch opened and a smaller woman stepped out. Smaller than I remembered, and her neck hung loosely.

'It's you.' She stared at me. 'Come in for shortbread when you have the fine thing done and in the truck. I'll start on them now.' She looked over my shoulder, over my head, and squinted. Then she shook her head gently and with a wave, disappeared inside the porch to the kitchen.

I couldn't help turning, looking behind me, and I saw a flash of orange. *Patrick*, I thought, then did my own gentle head-shake. Patrick wasn't here. He was three thousand miles away.

The orange I saw was the raincoat Dad was holding out to me. 'Here,' he said. 'Put this on. It's one of Patrick's.'

I took it, wondered how many rubber coats Dad has kept, all for different sizes of a rainy day. I slid my arms through the crackly sleeves – it was an older model – and as a reflex, pushed my hands into the pockets. There were mittens. Or rather, there was one. One big scruffy mitten. I thought I heard a laugh then, and a voice, like Patrick's.

Not staring out the window this time, are you?

I looked up to see Dad, to connect him with the voice, but he had already started out across the lumpy green yard behind the house, and I knew he hadn't spoken.

No, I'm not staring out the window. What happened to the other mitten?

Of course, there was no answer. Patrick never was keen on answers, any more than I was on questions. What bits of these seasonal tree journeys I'd gleaned from him over the years, had been just that: bits, crumbs. I kept my curiosity close.

December was like most on the coast. Grey mist left everything wet and it mizzled as I followed my father to the deep cut on one side of the green, filled with water. He followed the cut until he found the rough board that led over. The earth had grown hummocks that caught both ends of the board, and the wood was so rotting old, that I slipped and would have fallen to the water, except he grabbed my elbow and pulled me to the other side.

The grass was gone. We were in bog. My feet sank, and we were surrounded by forgotten blueberry bushes, fallen water-logs. Shallow-rooted cottonwoods moved over our heads, and the wind brought us raindrops that were waiting in the elbows of their branches. I pulled up my hood, fastened the top button, but I was too late and could feel water halfway down my back and soaking a damp spot on my shirt.

'Hard to chug through these damned blueberry trees, isn't it?' Dad yelled from ahead.

The bushes were trees, high on either side of me, and I followed his path, where he'd trampled them to the ground.

'Course nobody has tended these for a long time, nobody does anything here.'

[93]

To our right and over that same cut ditch, I caught a glimpse of other blueberries, lined and cultivated, the stalks a dark fallow winter red.

'How about this one?'

And while I was lagging and wet, I looked at the pine he pointed out and thought of Mum, even then laying out the boxes of ornaments, her mother's treetop star, and I shook my head.

He really is a nincompoop, isn't he? I almost giggled. The word had been one of our favourites. I'd forgotten about it, but it came back to my thoughts as smoothly as Patrick did. Nincompoop. I wet my pants once over that word.

Dad was standing, examining a tree. He turned to me as I walked up.

He'll never learn, will he? You gotta take time for the right tree. You can't take the first one you see.

Dad was watching me.

'It has no branches,' I pointed out.

'Well, we like 'em a little bare.' He set the saw to the bark — my brother's handsaw — and I realized then that he was breathing heavily. I sat on a log, tucking the bottom of my jacket between me and the soggy bark.

'You can't take the first one you see,' I said.

He looked up from the saw. 'That's what Patrick always says.'

'I remember him telling me. Sit down for a minute, Dad.'

He shook his head and put one hand high on the trunk of the standing tree and rested there. 'You think this one won't do?'

'Mum won't like it.'

'We can put it in the corner.' He peered up one side.

'That tree would need a three-sided corner to hide its bare spots. Sit down, Dad.'

He shook his head again, moved on, pushing, pulling the

thicket from his path, stomping the branches into the ground to clear my way, and he muttered words about trees of the past and other words I couldn't hear. Perhaps they were the words of conversations he'd shared with Patrick.

I wanted to stop him, keep him from talking, until his breath became even, but instead I quick-marched after him, my steps high as a child's to keep from tripping.

I was glad for Mum's boots; mine would have been soaked a quarter mile back. I had to watch the ground for other ditches – low points really – where the bog dropped away and leaked. I looked up after circling one such trap, looked for the mustard of Dad's toque, but it was gone.

I wouldn't be a child, crying out. I would follow the broken line he left behind.

When I did catch up to him, he was resting his backside on a fallen jack pine. Not sitting, just propped up, with his heels dug in. When I saw him like that I wished I had slowed. He could have used a few more minutes.

'I'd like to ease up a bit.'

He made some effort to twist his mouth into an expression of minor disgust. He was breathing too hard to speak.

I couldn't look at him then, so I turned to the way we'd come. 'We've come quite a way.'

'We have.' He gulped.

'Maybe we should have cut that first tree.'

'No, you were right. Mum wouldn't like it.' He lifted his right hand and quickly released and caught the saw. 'Let's go.' He strode off again.

Old fool.

I shivered – with the cold, the damp, I told myself.

How come you never asked Dad before? If you could come for the tree with us?

He – you – never asked me.

Can't always wait to be asked. I've told you that before.

I thought you meant other times.

It's always other times, isn't it, sister?

I remembered the angry look on Patrick's face when he was explaining his transfer to Sudbury, and three times Mum had said, 'Can't you find another position in Vancouver?'

It's just as I said it was, isn't it.

We came upon a knot of jack pines, eight or nine, and by the time we'd examined each, held it to Mum's standards, shaken our heads – toque and hood – his breathing had finally slowed and I'd pushed my questions and my fear to the gumboot toes.

We went off again and I tried not to hear his breathing. I concentrated on my own, made the passing out, the taking in of air, louder than it had to be.

Then I saw it. Deep green, shaped, not too many branches, not bare, one spindle perfect, waiting for the star.

Dad looked at it and his eyes lighted, dimmed. 'It's off the allowance,' he said. He waved the saw to some indistinct line of scrubby grasses and browned vines.

For a moment I thought how easy it would be. Then I imagined a four-lane where I stood, filled with Richmond rush: to the city; from the airport; the mall; to house-boxes. Beside the road would be this proud pine.

'Too bad.' Dad shifted away from that line. I knew he didn't see it as I had, and I knew he had very particular rules for occasions such as this, and didn't need to spend time deliberating.

'We'll find something soon,' he said. 'We always do.'

We always do.

Go, Patrick, I muttered. *Beat it.*

Why, Maid Marion, that's a first.

There was silence in my head.

Dad was moving, moving, out of sight. The brush seemed thicker, the bog deeper, and when I again caught up to him, he was standing – though not still – looking at another group of pines.

'Must be one in here,' he muttered, and began to circle. 'Must be.'

'This one.' He pointed to a forty-foot tree, again bare to the top.

'The top looks promising,' I ventured.

He set the saw to the bark. The smell of raw pine split the air.

'I could do that.'

He didn't stop. 'You do what?'

'Saw.'

He didn't answer. He worked the saw into a routine of one-two, one-two, one-two.

'I could take a turn,' I said.

One-two, one-two, one-two.

'Stand back,' he said.

I did, and watched it fall with a sodden thud.

He held the saw behind him as he hurried over – hunter to kill – to find the second cut. He used the saw, end over end, to measure.

'How long is the saw?' I asked.

He seemed surprised at my question, and hesitated. Did he have to remember the number? 'Eighteen inches.'

He'd lost count. He had to begin again. He counted, 'One, two, three, four, five, six ... nine feet, and the star.'

'Let me,' I said, and he didn't touch me, he didn't even say no, but he turned his back, his heavy shoulders were squared to me, so that he might as well have said No, and his elbow moved with inhuman force.

He picked up the heavier end of our tree and began to drag it, back the way we'd come, not stopping to look and find openings or paths free of strewn trees. He moved in a straight line.

I ran, picked up the other end, wondered for the quickest moment if I could carry the tree by myself. But I almost left a boot in the gnarled joints of a fallen limb, and had to twist my ankle to be free. Still he moved, breathing and head down.

It wasn't always like this, Patrick, not like this. He's older now.

I tried to keep my head above the needles. 'To your left,' I shouted. 'There's a clear path.'

He did hear me, because he swerved. The turning trunk almost overthrew me. He so quickly covered the yards to where the cottonwoods and vines tangled.

When he stopped, it was so sudden that I continued my pace with his old rhythm and needles broke the skin of my bare hands, a branch scraped my leg where my mother's boot ended.

He didn't even cry out. He leaned forward into a branch – that I saw – and when he stood, there was blood running from his forehead. He reached to touch it. Looked at his fingers with their bit of red. Raised his arm to wipe at it. Lowered his arm.

He had dropped his end of the tree. He folded his knees to pick it up again and when he unfolded, he stood for a long moment before his steps sagged into the softness.

I suppose I could have said something about it being my fault. I had suggested this route when he'd been so set on his, but he didn't seem to require an apology. Nor an anxious word. So I spoke none.

We'd not gone far, when he stopped, looked around. 'This way,' he motioned to the right, and I might have heard a question mark in his words.

He made another turn, stopped. He sat on a stump, the trunk cradled in his arms. He curled over it.

I put my end to the ground and waited.

It was another while before he went on, wending a path. The afternoon was growing winter dark when we came at last to the rotting board. I would have missed it, but my father's head was down, tracking his steps, and he saw the black-grass hummocks. He turned his back to the board-bridge, carrying the tree in front of him, and he felt for each footstep in the dark.

I could see the gash on his forehead. Not a large wound. The bleeding had stopped.

We crossed the yard slowly, guided by Mrs Sanders' porch light.

He opened the back of the truck and fed the tree into it, the spindle-top poking out the door of the canopy.

I walked to the passenger door, as he stood behind the truck and wrestled with his rain gear, threw it into the back, came round to my side, reached into the glove box for the towel that was there.

Mrs Sanders' storm door scraped open.

'Hot rum?' she asked.

Dad rubbed the towel over the blade of the saw. He didn't look up. He would climb into the driver's side and we would drive away, back home to Mum, waiting. It would be one more Christmas, though this time my brother wouldn't be there.

Dad put the saw behind the seat and handed me the towel.

I put my hand out for the towel, but I didn't take it.

'Hot rum?' My voice rose with the final word.

I looked at my Dad, his lines, his Beethoven brows, his eyes that turned down slightly, his teeth with crooked smile. His face, like mine.

He moved away, his boots crunched through gravel. I closed the glove box and looked up to see his foot on her lowest stair, his wide hand gripping the railing.

Quitting Finn

THERE WERE RUMBLINGS. Rumblings were inevitable in a shop with almost thirty employees. Stephen had heard many in his time. He considered them birth pains. So many of the hair shops that overpopulated the city had been spawned there. Almost every owner – around the corner and across town – had done their time with Finn.

The rumbling began, as most such rumblings did, in the senior staff room, where anyone who was not busy spent most of their time. Anyone who was not busy had something to grumble about, and the staff room was the room farthest from the receptionist's desk, where she – the receptionist – lowered her bosom over the appointment book, with its lists of clients and telephone numbers. There the book was quite safe and the woman had a curious way of rounding her shoulders, curving up and over the book as she spoke on the phone, allowing just enough space to pencil the appointment onto a line. When she stood to call to the back of the shop for an apprentice – *Annie! Mrs Joyce is here!* – her hand, with its metallic-pink hooks, spread over the page. There was only one time during the week when she was not there. And that was Saturday. Early Saturday morning, when Stephen was happy in spite of himself and when he forgot about being old and the possibility of being forgotten.

He might even sing then, at least until Dermot entered the shop. Dermot would sneak in from the alley to hide in the laundry room and light a Gitane. At the first curl of smoke, Stephen ceased to sing and Saturday – real Saturday – began. By ten o'clock, he would be red-faced and wrenching his earring and refusing Dermot's last-minute clients. Dermot's clients were always last-minute. They were as impulsive and compulsive as he – clients always mirror their chosen one. Dermot was a thorn in Stephen's crown, for certain, but there were others.

Finn. Finn whom Stephen loved. For surely seventeen years of working life was a form of love. The form that Stephen was most familiar with. And not for a moment had Finn loved Stephen in return. Some day he would though. The day would come when Finn did for Stephen what he'd done for no one else. Finn would love Stephen and never forget him.

Finn would fire Stephen.

Stephen worked on, counted his thorns, raged, and at night walked Robson Street and spat on the windows of other shops so that when the time came, there would not be a road left to him in the business. He made sure that Finn knew of his midnight deeds. When Finn's love came, it would be real and would set him free.

He couldn't quit, though he threatened to. If he quit he would be forgotten. And if Finn's wife – Susan – fired him ... no, he didn't want that. Susan was capable of firing. She had before.

Then Stephen would have to pack his bag: the crochet hooks – his number ten, fine, so pointed. Stephen kept it for those who'd not been highlighted elsewhere, those who did not know that having one's hair hook-pulled through the three hundred holes of a rubber cap was not supposed to be full of pain. Those who thought beauty had a price. Finn's clients.

And Stephen would pack his favourite tail-combs, the borrowed brushes, his collection of Band-Aids. No one else kept Band-Aids, and haircutters were always in need, especially the juniors and the apprentices on training nights – mornings after, there was a noticeable decrease in supply. They would miss his Band-Aids when he was gone.

Finn's wife would claim his corner of the mezzanine and redecorate with dollar-a-roll wallpaper. She would probably put in the air-conditioning he'd been asking for, for God-knows-how-long, and that would be it.

Rumblings began in the belly, and first showed with a belch. Stephen considered belching rude, except in a lover – then it was familial – and it had been some time since he had had one of those. He particularly disliked belching in the monthly staff meetings.

But Dermot belched. That is, he put words to feelings that should have been left to the staff room.

He complained about the coffee deduction.

When someone said something about the coffee deduction, the words had nothing to do with the drink; it did mean that the speaker was entertaining ideas of taking leave. Entertaining with champagne and red-silk robe and feather slippers on one's feet, Stephen fancied.

Dermot brought up the matter and several others said, quietly, that they agreed. Cal spoke loudly against; he was hoping to be manager someday.

Coffee deduction was a five-dollar charge on each pay cheque. It separated those who were happy from those who were not. It was brilliant. It must have been Susan's idea. To keep Finn from tossing and turning over malcontents and force him to remember her at night. Stephen shuddered when he pondered living with Susan. But he could imagine what it was to live with Finn.

This coffee thing, was how Dermot put it. *Yeah,* murmured three others: backup vocalists. They could have been sharing a microphone, Stephen thought. Hips to the left, hips to the right. *Ooooooooo.*

O bloody hell – not the coffee thing. Lucille sucked on her cigarette, her cheeks hollow and artificially blushed. She'd been at the shop as long as Stephen and had no plans to leave. None that Stephen knew of. She wrote to Ann Landers and often answered her own letters.

Finn sighed so gently.

Cal, manager of the future, said, *Now then, the apprentice program.*

So they moved on, but without Dermot and the backups. One apprentice shifted his weight as he stood against the wall so that he leaned closer to the mutineers, and Stephen knew which side he was with.

Stephen removed his glasses and peered through the lenses for dust, but really he was watching his Annie. Which was her camp? She was in those tights again – he'd warned her about those tights: black couldn't always be counted on with thighs like hers – and she was wearing a long pirate shirt. The shirt was good, he thought. She had a ring in her nose. That was good too. Or was she easily led? Led to what? Her freedom, as he hoped for his?

Annie was making the move from apprenticing to the floor. Finn had told the receptionist to see to it that Annie had an occasional client on Saturday or on Friday night. It was the adolescent stage – a dreadful in-between thing. Like having sex with someone and having to go home to your mother. Already Annie had had clients return. Stephen was proud. He imagined she looked like him, could have passed for the daughter he'd never had. She wasn't flamboyant like some, but people trusted her, and that was something. Her work was solid and intuitive. She would be too, if she trusted herself.

Stephen couldn't tell Annie that he was afraid she would be eaten up, that she would become a cokehead in another downtown shop, and return from her weekends some time on Wednesday, or she'd own a *Hair* franchise in Smithers.

Annie was naturally – or unnaturally – good with

understanding hair colouring. It was instinctive, and really she would have been best to pursue work as a technician and follow Stephen's path, but when she asked him, he said no. He said it jokingly, because he knew that if he did, she wouldn't ask again. She wouldn't dare if she thought he didn't take her seriously. Of course she cried, but apprentices were always in tears.

No, he thought. Annie must keep her options open, because if she specialized she would be eaten even sooner than he had predicted.

So where was she? Whose camp? He watched.

The meeting disbanded as usual. Finn climbed out of his chair mid-sentence and disappeared into the staff room. Those who were sitting on the counter that encircled the room stood, and cigarettes were butted and hands batted the smoke in the air – the shop was officially non-smoking. The senior stylists headed down the open stairs to their clients waiting below. The juniors clustered in their room, a cluster of angry impotent minimum-wage-earners. Each knew that they were replaceable and each believed that at some time they would be the superior hairdresser, and travel: to London – Sassoon was still a name, though the man himself had sold it; Italy looked good; there was always Paris. Then they'd come back and show everyone in this one-horse place.

Stephen heard and walked in on them, tossing his head, snorting, pawing the air. And they laughed uneasily. They wanted to be heard, and they didn't. Stephen knew they feared him, and so they should. He worked for their fear as he worked for his freedom.

But the apprentices never said anything. Not anything that would matter, and not to Finn. It didn't pay large dividends to draw their tears, though he'd done so with every one of them. But Stephen knew a bit of misery in an employee is an exponential thing. He knew numbers in his own way.

Rumblings always ended in some little sadness. He would miss Michelle – one of Dermot's backups. Michelle was good for a tickle. But – Stephen stood at the fore of his mezzanine, watching below – he would be glad to see Dermot go.

He pondered Annie, but as he did, she passed from under his floor, and he heard her hum bars of 'La Vie en Rose'. Not hum really, but as he himself did it, slightly opened mouth, a little rasp, *do do-do-do do-do-do*, and he saw her point her toe as she swept cut hair under the hinged door-flap beneath the stairs. That was his girl.

His smile turned vicious as he looked towards the front and the broad back of the receptionist. There was Dermot skulking by the appointment book, hovering for a chance – a quarter-half-chance to glimpse a client's name and telephone number. He'd given himself away with the coffee deduction. Now he was blatantly trying to collect a client list. Fool. Did he think that Finn wouldn't notice?

Stephen thought to take a wee stroll by the desk, drop a hello to the receptionist. They had no reason not to be friends – he didn't depend on her for clients. But she had stepped away by the time he reached the desk, though Dermot lurked still.

Subtle, whispered Stephen. He reached behind Dermot and squeezed the back of his thigh, under his cheek. *Subtle*.

Dermot turned away as the receptionist neared. *It's impossible*, he said, and those were probably the only honest words he'd ever uttered to Stephen.

Dermot moved to the washroom, possibly for a snort, and Stephen noticed Finn stepping back from his client, scowling after him. Then Finn turned and looked directly at Stephen. He smiled at Stephen as he hadn't since Christmas Eve 1989, and that had been eggnog and rum.

Stephen, said the receptionist, sliding into her seat. She bosomed the book and Stephen kissed her cheek.

You can be anything you want to be, he said to her and waved as he left. He knew she liked it when he said that. Made her think all those night-school courses were not for naught.

It had come to him: with Finn's smile, it had come to him. He two-stepped to the washroom, and there raked his nails across the door. *Saturday morning, tomorrow,* he whispered, *Saturday, seven o'clock. I'll scratch yours, you scratch mine.*

The door opened without a sound and Dermot reached for Stephen's belt, would have pulled him inside, but Stephen slapped the hand. *Scratch. I said, scratch.*

Dermot looked confused.

There are many ways to scratch. There are other things in this world, said Stephen, his head high.

Dermot's face smoothed. He even smiled. *You'd know all about that.*

Friday night the shop was open until ten. Susan came in at six and took over the receptionist's place at the front. At nine, after the last client had come in, she would take the appointment book, close it, and lock it in the shallow drawer.

Just before nine, Stephen brought his client downstairs, seated her in Michelle's chair, slowly pulled a comb through her fresh perm. She was a nice client, he thought, idly watching her in the mirror. Plain, but nice.

Stephen looked for Michelle. He liked to hear the comments of the stylists. *Wonderful curl, Stephen. Lovely colour. Such natural highlights.*

Then Michelle was there at his side, looking at him in the mirror. He breathed a waft of Gitane from her – she must have been in the alley with Dermot. Her sly smile told him so even before she spoke. *Dermot says we must thank you. Why you're doing this, I can't imagine.*

How far did her voice carry? Stephen looked for Finn. Was he watching? Had he heard? *My pleasure,* Stephen answered her.

Finn was calling for an apprentice to see his client to the

door, but from the corner of his eye, Stephen watched him and knew he'd seen, he'd heard.

A feeling rushed through him, a feeling of faithlessness and victory.

Michelle was pulling her fingers through new curls. *Nice, Stephen,* she said.

Yes.

In the senior staff room he was glad for the cold weather. It was satisfying to throw a scarf around his neck, over a shoulder, and don a hat.

The staff room wasn't large, just enough for a ragged wicker loveseat, four old chairs, a fridge, an orange door to an outside stairway, and a green door that led to Finn's office. Once Stephen had been behind that door. Once, seventeen years ago, when he'd accepted Finn's job offer. Everyone was in that room once.

Stephen buttoned only the upper buttons on his coat. He liked when the wind down Robson pushed and pulled and made the coattails billow like a great flapping sail. Then he thought about going away somewhere.

As he sailed down that sidewalk in the city that was almost his, a vision, like a partner, danced before him.

The green door.

He thought to knock at it, try the knob. He walked faster, almost running, as if to plunge through, and he was in his building, in the elevator and home, still with the green door. It was close, so close he could show it to Ms Swanson on his wall, in her silver frame.

Look, Gloria. Finn's door. I'm going to go through that door. Sometime next week. Even tomorrow. And what will he say. What will he say.

Stephen was pulling his scarf from his neck as he spoke, getting the long strip of wool caught in his hat as he hurried to unwrap himself.

He mixed his usual vodka-and-pepper trick and placed a glass of wine on the empty bookshelf in front of Gloria. *To us,* he said, and their glasses clinked before Stephen whirled away. *What will he say, what will he say.* In a deepened and slow voice, he answered: *Stephen, I'm sorry, but I'm going to have to let you go. What you have done is intolerable.* He turned to Gloria. *Will that be it?* He wouldn't dare say, *You're fired, or, I must fire you – no – I mustn't even think such a thing. But, I'm-going-to-have-to-let-you-go. Oh, pillow talk.* Vodka splattered to the floor as he spoke.

Stephen was exhausted. One button still kept his coat with him and he sat in one of two big chairs in the room. *It will be,* he murmured over and over, forgetting the woman on the wall. *It will be.*

He sipped vodka and as he raised the glass to his lips, he smelled ammonia, realized he'd almost stopped smelling it. Peroxide and perm solutions. Next week his body would begin to expel the dreadful stuff. It had been with him for so long. He dipped his fingers in the vodka and slowly put each to his mouth.

Dermot and Michelle waited for him at the front door, stamping their feet in silly shoes. *Do you shop together too?* Stephen asked as he put his key to the hole. *What about the others?* He reached for the main switch. He knew exactly where it was in the dark.

We'll get the names for all of us, Michelle said. They were already huddled over the desk, waiting for him to fetch the book from the drawer. He had that key as well.

He unlocked the drawer and moved away, to the far side of the desk, lest Dermot take it into his head to thank him in a form other than words.

Thanks, said Michelle, and Dermot smiled like an evil thing.

Stephen hurried upstairs remembering the words, *It will*

be, and he didn't sing that Saturday morning, though he hummed snippets of something from his head.

The early apprentice came in and began to fold towels for the day. Stephen shouted for him to make coffee instead, and then sat at his own desk. *My last Saturday. Maybe I will never work another Saturday in my life. I will be like all those other people who don't work on Saturday.* He opened the drawers, one at a time, and closed each before he opened the next. Then he opened them all at once, and closed them in quick succession. Except the last two stuck. He wiggled them as only he knew how and slammed them shut. *Next week.*

He checked his watch. Twenty minutes to eight. Finn would come through the staff room door any time between quarter to and the hour itself. It was time to keep watch. He went downstairs for the cup of coffee that the apprentice had forgotten to bring to him, circled the desk – *I'll be on guard* – and marched up the stairs, where he hovered in the staff room, waited for Finn's footfalls outside the entrance door. He touched the intercom button for the desk, then moved to the vantage point of his mezzanine as Dermot and Michelle hurried to close the book, shove it back into the drawer, lock it. The deed was done.

Did Finn catch Stephen's wide and satisfied smile? He could only hope. Finn had seen Michelle's sly look of the night before. Stephen was certain of it.

Now.

Finn couldn't miss Michelle slipping the key back into the pocket of Stephen's loose cardigan.

How much more did he need? Finn was a man of subtlety – that was why he'd never had to fire anyone. They did it to themselves.

The shop was filling now. The receptionist took her place at the front, apprentices came in. There was Annie. In a black empire waist. Good. Stephen nodded at her. He lifted his apron from the back of his chair and brought it down over his head, around his neck, tied it in back, and hurried down the stairs to see to his first client. One of Finn's, she was. One who wanted natural highlights.

Go easy with the crochet hook, Finn said softly as he passed.

So Finn knew the thing that Stephen did with his crochet hook. A thin sliver of ice was being slid into the centre of Stephen's vertebrae. Where his spinal cord should have been, was the thought that passed through his mind. How could Finn have seen that broken skin, perhaps inflicted more pain with his comb, how could he have discovered, and not fired Stephen then?

The client went home, shoulders aching with tension, and with an unmarked scalp.

It was an odd day, even more so for a Saturday. Employees were gentle with each other, shared bits of their lunches. Michelle gave enough tip money to an apprentice to buy bottles of iced tea for the apprentice as well as for herself. Stephen watched from his mezzanine. He had time to watch. Dermot didn't have any last-minutes for him that day.

Just as misery was an exponential thing, so too was the ease that came with knowing one had not long in an unhappy place.

Stephen looked to the front desk. The chair was empty. The receptionist on a rare excursion to the loo? There'd been times Stephen wondered if she had a bladder.

There was Annie. At the desk, with a hand on the book. Pointing, he could see. To Dermot beside her.

The ice sliver was in place.

He would have lost her anyway, he consoled himself. He would be gone from this place by next week, and he would have lost her anyway. What was the difference if she stayed or if she left? What did it matter to him?

He checked his watch. Four forty-six. Lucille could take

his last client. He would ask her. She owed him. He'd never asked her for anything.

She said yes, and he went to the staff room for his coat. There was no one there on that late Saturday afternoon and he approached the green door. How he would have liked to lay a dusty bootprint into it or a fine globule of spit. He'd have to wait until next week for his time on the other side of the green.

He did not leave through the upstairs entrance, but rather plunged down the front stairs. He stopped midway to call to Annie, *Rinse my highlight cap and don't forget to powder it.* She was too busy attending a client, with two more in chairs waiting for her. She turned wild – even angry – eyes to him as he called. He did not look at her again as he crossed the length of the shop and he made a show of wrapping his scarf around and around his neck and his elbow struck Finn even as he had the bloody piece of wool over his face. He pulled it down, into its place, and pushed his hat on, met Finn's smile. Finn leaned into him, his scissors and comb held to his chest. Finn rolled his eyes in Dermot's direction and opened his mouth. Stephen tasted his breath, of no lunch and too much talk. *Glad you're with us.*

Fervent Charity

... take whom thou lovest, and get thee
into the land of Moriah; and offer her
there for a burnt offering upon one of
the mountains which I will tell thee of ...

Jo's mother was a woman whose body was not enough to hold her soul. Her soul needed more, so she found a building in the Cariboo, off the highway, on a hill among some dry pines where between prayered words there were the rattles of snakes.

A curious building. Hardly a church. More a home for fowl, topped with quaint cupola. Hardly a spire. But it was surrounded by thin air and in the shadows and wind, the broken branches that snapped underfoot, in the hot summer smell of bursting pines, her mother seemed to feel at peace.

She looked upward and said it was their mountain, said she had been moved of God to this place.

Every morning, she climbed the hillside and asked Jo to come with her, but Jo said no, and stayed close to the building, a place of peeling siding boards, two-by-four studs, no insulation, and water stains – brown, brown, darker brown stretching circles from the rain, so rare. An outhouse was off the back porch, a tiny room with warped lines of sun lighting the joints of thin plywood walls, and on the door a crescent moon cut-out.

A summer church, her mother said. 'People will stop on their way to some other place and maybe – just maybe, Jo – they'll change direction.' Her mother had such hope in her eyes, when she spoke; Jo felt she could almost touch her then.

They slept back to back beneath their quilt, and stayed in the room off the main, because Jo's mother wouldn't let them live in the sanctuary. 'It is the place of the Spirit,' she said. And she swept it with a broom from the corner, swept it clean in the early morning when the wind was low.

There was a wood stove in the room, and that was how people discovered them. The owner of the property first, in a flatbed truck, pulled close to the front door and shouted: 'Gypsies! Tramps! This is private property.' Then he saw the Bible that Jo's mother kept on the platform, saw the crackly paper picture of Christ on the far wall, and a smile came to his face – at least to the half of his face that Jo could see through her crack in the wall. Her mother poured boiling water into the teapot unalarmed, as if she heard nothing.

'Hello?' the man began again. He stepped out across the sanctuary and the floor sagged with his heavy soles.

Jo's mother silently placed enamel mugs and the teapot on a tray – she could be so still when she wanted to be – and glided, robes flowing behind her. A white dress, billowing. Jo loved to watch her mother move like that, though she knew her mother would someday leave her the same way.

Her mother swept through the doorway and stopped the man from going further.

'Do have some tea.' She went past him. 'Not here, of course. On the porch.'

At the door, she looked straight at him. 'I believe your truck is in our path.'

'I suppose I could do something 'bout that.'

Jo rather liked his unused growl. She crept out of their room and passed along the edge of the sanctuary, stopped just behind the wall by the door.

There was a loud roar of engine and the sanctuary filled with exhaust. There was a crunch of pine as he backed into a tree. Then Jo heard their steps on the porch.

'Watch that board.' Her mother's voice could be so mild.

There was a crack of wood, followed by an exclamation – more of breath than anything – from the man. The beginnings of some word he stopped at. There was the sound of pouring.

Jo had to hiccup. She kept her mouth closed, though the back of her throat wrenched. She put her hand over her mouth. How did her mother keep so silent? She held her breath. Made for better listening.

'Where's the water from?'

'The pump.' Her mother's voice was smooth.

'That pump hasn't watered in four years. I haven't had rain all season.'

There was a pause.

'Call me Ruth.'

'Name's Paddy.' Another pause, then a loud slurp with no apology. Her mother wouldn't like that, but she'd forgive him.

'That there's my land.'

Jo imagined he waved his arm then.

He spoke again. 'This land too. Part of mine.'

'Yes, the land.' There was a clink as Jo's mother settled her mug onto a plate, as if it were cup on saucer. She rolled round the word *land* like it was the world and as big, and the man was a long time replying.

Jo crept closer to the door, but at the first movement of her foot a floorboard was angry.

'Josepha. Come meet our brother.'

The door was closed now, but there was a panel missing from the lower half. Jo sat on the floor and put her head between the slats of moulding.

Sometimes she didn't recognize her mother. This was one of those times. Her features, eyes, cheekbones, could widen. Her ears could stretch. Her smile was a sad thing. Nostrils like a horse afraid.

The scar that ran from the edge of her lip to her jaw was familiar, though. Always there, always thin, always white. Her mother had been born with it, it seemed.

The man was with his back to Jo, but he turned.

'Name's Paddy.'

'This man says he is the owner of all this,' her mother said, poured out more tea. She kept her eyes down. 'Says we can stay here.'

The man, Paddy, raised a hand. 'I don't recall ...'

She put the mug in his hand. She looked brighter. She could do that, too. And bigger.

'I'm bringing good news. If any man thirst, Mr Paddy.'

'Sure could use some good news,' he said. 'Been dry round here of late.'

'Probably been dry around here a long time. You haven't noticed.'

He was back at his tea again. 'You got any milk for this?'

'No. We haven't any milk.' She rattled the tea things back onto the tray. It was time for him to leave. She pushed the door in, almost on Jo, who scrambled.

The man drove off with a radio on, fiddle and bass, in the raised dust, and Jo went to visit the wound on the pine. She touched the opened yellow.

'Jo?' called her mother. 'Help me with this door. Off its hinges it'll be fine. People will know we're here.'

Jo held the door while her mother wedged a screwdriver into a hinge, shoe-battered it – rusted, painted over – till it gave in to her.

That morning, she was late going up the mountain. Jo watched her ascent and the scattering of pine needles from her path.

Some mornings she turned almost as soon as she was there, and returned, her body sideways to the mountain, dropping down with her legs long and snapping like a goat's.

Other times she stayed till after the middle of the day was past.

That morning, Jo caught sight of her at the open space near the summit, through the black limbs of the trees. She was standing, just standing, and spreading sunlight reached her through a tear in the cloud. Jo shivered.

Paddy was back the next day with a crock of milk.

He set the milk on the porch. He left the truck engine rumbling, music on, and Jo crept close to the sounds, the dancing sounds, sounds that set the insides of her ears humming and her feet twitching. She crept not far from her mother, though.

'Where's my door?' Paddy demanded.

'The Lord doesn't like doors, unless they're open,' said Jo's mother, and she hoisted the crock to her hip, stood there, feet wide, like she was holding a big baby.

'You hopin' people'll come to this place?'

'Maybe a few. With encouragement.'

'You mean with a shove.' He stalked back to the truck, noticed Jo there with the radio, but he said nothing, climbed into his seat. Then he looked at her and turned the volume slowly right. Jo began to sway. She tried to keep herself still, but Paddy caught her, grinned, closed the door, was gone.

Sunday morning there was no wind. Jo's mother took the twelve strings of her guitar and sang about joy, and Jo's voice followed behind, though her voice was nothing she liked and she kept her sound low. The air was thin again, as it always was on her mother's best days, and the sound carried surely to the highway. A car pulled off the highway.

Three people – two men, one woman – sat on the pew, and Jo's mother spoke. About the Spirit. God. Jesus, his son. But mostly the Spirit. You could know the Spirit, her mother said.

The Spirit was in her mother's soul, Jo knew. She wondered if it slipped in through the scar at her jaw, and if it could leave the same way.

Though it troubled her, Jo liked when her mother talked about the Spirit – made Jo think she could know him some-day, too.

Jo never asked her mother where they were going to be in winter. The summer was so hot in the church, she knew winter would be cold. She had known walls like that, and what it was not to have a door.

The rancher brought milk to them, eggs, flour, coffee even Jo learned to drink heavy and black. Perhaps he kept hoping that that woman, bigger and brighter every time he saw her, would have something to do with making it rain. Perhaps he needed a woman like Jo's mother. Needed her big and bright. 'When's it gonna rain, Elijah?' he'd say.

She would wave her fist in the air. Point to it with her other hand and laugh.

'A cloud the size of a fist, and you'll be a contented man.'

Others came: saw the smoke from the stovepipe, heard the song, saw Jo's mother moving up the slope, noticed Jo picking pine cones from the ground.

She bordered the porch with those cones, their smooth splayed brown teeth, always with the hook on the end in the middle. She came to know how to pick them up, how to avoid the hook, and she spent the morning hours there, working the cones into circles or into story-patterns like the stars.

More people came. They never lingered at the door, the way people did at other church buildings Jo had known, but they entered quickly, assuredly. Her mother was right about the door then. They left quickly, too, but that didn't seem to disturb Jo's mother: 'They're travellers,' she said.

There was only one pew, narrow and long across the sanctuary, in front of the tapering yellow-wood pulpit. Jo and her mother made another bench with bare boards: railings they removed from the back porch. They laid them on cut logs.

On the fourth Sunday, the seats were full.

The rancher came the day after, and seemed then as if he'd come for a report. 'Well, Ruth' – then – 'Reverend,' he added, and though he'd probably spent half his life with a piece of grass between his teeth, that Monday morning he seemed to have rehearsed this habit. He danced the tufty wheat-top as if he was a feather-mad bird preening. Perhaps he thought it made him appear that he didn't much care for Jo's mother and this little home she was making of someone else's.

'You've got my old place lookin' fine,' he said, his head nervous on his neck.

'Your place could use some paint.' Her voice was sharp. She could stand so still, not an itch in any place, hands loosely at her sides, eyes all like a lake of clouds.

Jo could be still too, when she was near her mother, but it was a small still.

The man had bones in his back though, and he said, 'Seems you're missin' some porch railin'.'

'Even God's people have asses, Rancher Paddy,' and she laughed. Which was not unusual, but always startling.

He paused, his eyes were gone for a moment. 'I got asses too. They're thirsty asses. Thought it was an ass carried the child's mother. Thought they shouldn't go without.' He turned away. 'Thought all kinds of ideas in my time,' he muttered, but his words carried clear.

'I hear you,' said Jo's mother.

The man turned back at the door of his truck, his hand there on the handle and he looked at her for a long time, her not flinching. Jo didn't like either of them very much just then.

Next day he came, angry-like, and threw the railings out of the sanctuary, threw the logs in Jo's direction, to be stacked again. He measured the pew that was there, and cut the wood he'd brought with him. The wood was good, with soft edges and few knots.

'Momma,' said Jo. 'When are you going to give the man his water?'

'He's not thirsty,' said Jo's mother.

One morning, Jo's mother slept long. Jo had pumped bitter water from the ground, washed, eaten the bread cooked flat on top of the stove, drunk the milk the man left for her, all in their little room, and still her mother slept.

'The sanctuary is holy,' her mother had told her. 'It is not for us to go into without purpose and a clean mind.'

When her mother was speaking there, Jo felt that was truth. It was the place of the Spirit. Other times when Jo had to pass through the sanctuary – to the porch, front or back to the outhouse with the moon door – then she tightened her bones, passed through with her eyes cast down.

Jo sat in the quiet of her mother's sleep. Her mother didn't breathe when she slept. Jo heard a whisper from the sanctuary. Perhaps just the wind through the open door, the cracks between the siding. She stood, wavered to the door, opened it.

For a moment she tasted bile, her feet were like leaden weights. Then she walked through the doorway over rough floorboards, stood between the pews. As she waited, a strange wind played through the doorway – scurried brittle leaves in for company, though Jo hadn't seen a tree with leaf for miles and days – and carried the finest clay dust. The wind left the leaves, the silt, in corners, in tiny drifts at the feet of the pews. Then moved on, through the back door, played the moon-hole like a guitar without strings, humming to itself, a child content.

Jo followed it, watched its trail, listened, returned to the sanctuary.

A great wheezing sound, like an aged person with miserable lungs: the sound of Jo's mother summoning her breath, awakening. The sound of her heaving herself upright.

She was standing in the doorway.

'What is it?' She came forward to Jo, and Jo saw that her eyes were closely set, her ears flat.

'What is it?' Her voice rose, and she held an arm across her face, but perhaps just to protect from the sunlight at a slant across the room.

'It's nothing, Momma.' That's what Jo said.

A clop of hoof. Another. A cow through the door.

Jo's mother's ears spread.

'What have you done?' Her voice had lowered again. She stepped towards the animal. 'Begone,' she said. 'Beast.'

The cow looked at her, feet shuffling, then turned, was gone.

'You too.' She turned on Jo, who scuttled.

The creek was dry, pine needles running in its narrow bed. The man was there, crouched, fingers curled in the needles.

'Your mother. Does she know 'bout fervent charity? Seems to me I once heard 'bout fervent charity.' He ducked his head.

'I don't know, Mr Paddy,' Jo said. 'I expect she does. She's read the whole Bible right to Revelations, you know, *an hundred times,* she says.'

The man grunted. 'I think these needles is so dry you could light them afire just steppin' on them.' He rubbed a handful between his fingers and smoke curled through. He drew close to Jo, opened his fingers all of a sudden, laughed aloud. 'It's just the dust that makes it asmoke. Just the dust, girl.' He pulled on her hand, stretched her fingers, placed orange needles there. 'You try.'

She moved her fingers as she'd seen him. The needles pricked.

His breath was hot on her forehead. 'You believe your ma can do something for my rain?' He didn't wait for her answer, stood, pulled her to her feet, and set off.

'Got somethin' I want you to see.'

They walked until the sun was low, its thread about to snap. A cow was lying off a bit. 'Don't you go near.'

Jo didn't want to go near. She could hear its moans.

'You go back now,' said the man, after the animal was quiet and the body was a black shadow.

Jo went home, smelled her way.

Morning, a crock of milk, loose tea in a tin, brown eggs warm, and a piece of jerked beef, at the top of the two steps to the front porch.

Jo's mother spoke as she prepared breakfast. 'Truly this man is an hospitable one.'

Jo said, 'He has a dead cow.'

Her mother broke eggs into the pan.

'Something about rain, Momma,' Jo said.

Jo's mother said nothing, cooked, and when she had cooked, she ate. When she had eaten, she stood.

'I will return.' She did not ask Jo to come with her. She put a wide straw sun hat on her head, bundled kindling into a sack, pulled the burlap up over her back, and was gone.

Jo sat for some time, still, as if listening to her mother's footfalls between the pines, climbing her mountain. She closed her eyelids, shivered, and when she opened them she saw first the plate and mug of her mother. Then she saw the mug had water in it.

Jo climbed through the window of the little room, the plate caught in the elastic waist of her skirt, the mug of water handled in her fingers. She went round to the porch, set the mug and plate down, and set herself to work on the arranging of her cones. First, those that were closed so tightly, and then the brave cones, alternating, circling the water. She dipped her hand into the water and with her fingers, traced the earth, by the porch step. Clay gathered on her fingers and she took up a handful, poured a little water into it, mixed it, moulded it, pulled at it, till a head showed itself, horns, ears, legs, a fly-chasing tail: a cow.

The sun swung up over the roof and she waited. Then the shadow of the place stretched out in front of her. She thought of her mother's fist.

Without headlights, the man came. The dust hadn't settled and he stood in front of her, something shiny with moon in his hand.

'It's for you. Music,' he said, and Jo took it from him. It was wood and silver. Fit even in her hand, a slim shining box of hollow teeth. She would have stayed there with it, with her cones and her cow of clay, but Paddy told her, No, move on, I have business here. So she took it to the truck, crawled up to the open bed, looking away. Sat with feet dangling. She blew a funny chord. Gently. Then pulling in, blowing out, moving it north and south in her hands. Each time a different sound. She almost forgot him.

The silver turned to a bar of gold. She held it out. Unlike anything she had ever seen.

'Look!' she cried to the man. She turned, saw the fire through the open doorway, heard the crackle, of pines remembering what it was to feel heat, remembering to open to the flame, to spit seed. She saw her mother come from the trees to the flames, white fabric billowing.

Momma.

Jo's mother turned, but then away. With hands high, she was gone into the sanctuary.

Something Blue

THOUGH NELLIE persuaded herself that she was not unhappy, one morning she awoke and discovered otherwise. She put her fingers to the cold outer layer of quilt, then retreated and thought.

She thought, *I'm tired of being alone. But even more, I'm tired of looking for someone and waiting for someone.*

She had been waiting, though of late, she rarely looked.

She curled her body under the quilts, stretched suddenly, pushed them away from herself all at once, felt the chill air. She reached for a long full skirt, shirt, vest, cardigan, warm socks for the cold wooden floor, and after coffee, honey and toast, she built a birdhouse. A feeder, really, with a large floor, wide sloping roof. She opened her file of newspaper clippings, found the diagram and photo she'd saved the spring before and for wood, she split an old apple crate.

Of course Sebastian heard her, hammering nails in the tiny backyard. He'd probably heard her sawing, but he came outside to witness her hammering.

'Nellie!' he shouted. He always shouted. 'What are you creating there?'

She imagined other neighbours' heads out of windows to see what they could. She held it up briefly.

'A bird feeder!' he announced. 'Well, you know about them....' He turned back to the door he'd left open.

'No, I don't. I've never had a bird feeder.'

'Really,' he said. 'You strike me as someone who would know everything about birds and feeding them.' He spoke over his shoulder.

She wondered why he thought that, but didn't ask.

She'd lived next to Sebastian for nine years. He wore too many Hawaiian prints in summer, shorts in late fall, indulged in magenta lights at Christmas, built plastic homes around his two living palm trees in terra cotta containers on either side of his carport. He took great delight in going out for the evening and returning early in the morning, with roars of Jaguar power and doors slamming. He was never out for the entire night. At about ten on Saturdays and Sundays, he would stroll onto his balcony, coffee in hand, and always that hair on his head. Though he must have been near fifty, his hair was so black, and was patterned with cowlicks and whorls, so that in the morning – and often at other times of day – it stood in every direction and mostly up. For work, and his evenings, he controlled it with something shiny and wet.

'What is it I should know about bird feeders?' she asked.

He was almost through the door.

'Once you start feeding the buggers, there's no stopping, you know.' His sliding door locked into position.

He was on his balcony when she took the feeder up to her own, and fastened it to the railing. Still in his blue robe, hair in a peak.

She felt dismay, finding him there. Though the townhouses were staggered and allowed for privacy, Sebastian seemed intent on thrusting his broad shoulders over the railing, over her basil and mint, into her home. Even when he was on his balcony with a woman, he would include Nellie in their conversation. Of course, she was able to hear every word, then he'd check with her: 'Isn't that so, Nel,' he'd say, or, 'How did that go again?' Sometimes she spied out of an upper-floor window to make certain that his balcony was empty, and hers safe.

'What kind of birds are you going to attract?' he asked. He looked as if he could step easily over the railing that separated them, with one stride.

'I don't know,' she said. 'I suppose I need some wild seed.'
She regretted the words.

'Sowing wild seed, are you?' His black eyes glowed. 'Or just wanting wild birds?'

'Here,' he said, leaving her standing on her balcony waiting for him as he disappeared into his living room. 'Here,' he said again as he came outside. He handed her a book. 'This was my mother's. Keep it.'

Nellie didn't hear sentimentality or grace in his voice. He didn't seem to want her thanks and she was happy he left before she opened it. *Birds of the West Coast*, it was, with a chapter on feeding. She left the book on the chesterfield.

The day was warming. She took off her cardigan and went to the store, bought a twenty-pound bag of mixed wild seed and a wide pan for water.

The bag should last until September, the woman at the store said, and she tried to talk Nellie into buying thistle seed and sunflower, but Nellie shook her head and returned home.

She set the seed out, filled the pan, and went into her home.

What an odd place, she found herself thinking as she stood in her living room. Though she'd never thought that before. Now she thought, *This home is not meant for one person. Not meant for two either, or a family of more. It is meant for visitors.*

The centre of the room was filled with the bulk of her mother's chesterfield, and her father's old chair and two matching chairs she'd bought for herself, for guests. The coffee table was big and square, for board games, if anyone still played them, and end tables were scattered everywhere.

Nellie had worked as a researcher since university, and her books were tucked on ugly shelves downstairs, and her papers were hidden in drawers in her study upstairs, though often she'd paused in the living-room doorway and thought how pleasurable it would be to have her desk there, before the wide glass doors, catching the morning sun as she worked.

That night she fell asleep on the chesterfield, as she had so often as a child, on a Sunday afternoon when the rest of her family was at the beach, or on December nights by the lighted tree, and the following morning she saw the first bird – a sparrow. Not a real sparrow of course, but a house sparrow. They find everything before other birds. Nellie read that much in the book. The brown and black-striped head attacked the tiny mound of seed, spread it over the wooden floor of the feeder and onto the balcony. Through the open French door, Nellie could hear seed scatter to the ground below. Then the bird flew away with the news.

Next door, on the balcony, Sebastian discussed bagels with a woman and raged about white or poppy seed: poppy were his favourite. The woman's voice hummed through and between his words, and finally Sebastian was quiet.

Nellie watered her herbs and watched them leave: the woman with a marching step and Sebastian silent, his hair shiny and restrained.

As he pulled away from the curb, Nellie couldn't hear the woman's words, but could see her lips moving behind the glass of the car door. The car went down the street without its usual roars.

So that was how to beat the man, Nellie thought. *Drone.*

But she had no desire to beat Sebastian, and so she finished her watering, set seed in the feeder, and returned to the house.

In July the days were hot and in the mornings the sparrows splashed, and ate greedily. At noon, Nellie would put out several handfuls of seed and refill the pan, and again at suppertime. She could see the sparrows in the fir by the street; in the heat of the day the tree was quite still as the birds moved in a comfortless shuffle. Every so often, briefly, they would skirmish, perhaps to create some bit of wind. It was too hot even for bugs, and the birds waited for the day to cool again to feed.

Nellie rid herself of several end tables, relocated her father's chair to her bedroom, and moved the bookshelves into the living room. She spent hours in that room and the sparrows came to know her movements, and she grew sensitive to theirs, and so it was that she forgot there were birds who weren't sparrows.

One morning there was a bird with a black hood and a cheering yellow beak, and at first she thought it was some kind of chickadee – her knowledge being the size of a grain of sand – and then she realized it was not, and she took the bird book from the shelf.

The bird was an Oregon junco, she discovered. She watched each morning for him and the Oregon junco seemed content with the wild seed. Others came, and as they did, she was forced to be still again. Other birds, she discovered, were not as curious or as brave as the sparrows, and would flee if she stood suddenly or looked directly at them.

'The juncos,' Sebastian nodded when, over the railing, he asked her what had been to her feeder, and she told him, and he said *juncos* so easily – as if he knew more of her new friends than she did. And he probably did, in his own loud, casual way, and that made her uncomfortable. She wanted to correct him, say *Oregon juncos,* but she didn't.

Chickadees began to come too. Black-capped chickadees, she learned, though she called them chickadees. They moved so quickly, never doubting their own bodies, and they plucked the sunflower seed from the mixed pile. They were so cautious of the sparrows, and circled, fluttered, never angry or defensive, just waiting. They were absurdly happy.

There was something satisfying to her simple judgements: sparrows, curious; juncos, self-assured; chickadees, happy.

Then came a nuthatch – red-breasted, Nellie found. The red-breasted nuthatch never let her know anything about him. He was quick and he didn't seem to like her feeder. He tap-danced the spine of the fir in his blue-grey uniform with the red umber cravat, and his made-up striped face, and he ignored her offerings.

Nellie tilted her head. 'Acknowledging your freedom, Mr Nuthatch,' she said.

He skittered sideways and she turned away from the window, went back upstairs to her desk.

Sometimes, when her work was done, she spread a blanket out on the warm floor of the balcony – near the wall adjacent to Sebastian's so that, if he looked, he wouldn't see her – and she watched the seagull silver high in the blue above her. Round and round. Sometimes a flock. Sometimes she felt she was with them, but often it was one up there circling and then she felt alone.

She found her job unsettling – it was a puzzle of perfect-fitting pieces, except there were too many pieces. She'd find the pieces, every one of them, and then she would disk them or box them or put them in the form her employer wanted, and that would be the end of it. She would rearrange her cupboard – all the pot handles to the right – or sort her cutlery tray or her linen closet, make sure everything was in order, and then she would look at her client list to find who was next. She was always busy. She was good at what she did.

And now that she'd made the decision not to look or wait for someone, she was truly free.

Late September there was a week of storm – wind and rain – and the sparrows made quick flights between the feeder and the blowing fir in which they huddled. One sparrow spent an entire morning sitting by the wide post in the feeder, to keep from the wind. His feathers were bunched and his shoulders protected his head. He didn't look at Nellie, though she was certain he knew she was there, passing her hands over her books. At ten, she realized she'd accomplished nothing.

Her older brother's son was coming by that afternoon, as he often did. She asked him if he would help to move her desk downstairs.

'Here?' he asked, looking around the living room.

'We'll have to move these two chairs,' was her answer.

'Where to?' he asked, hoisting a chair easily to his shoulder.

'Home – you take them,' she said. She knew he wanted to leave his parents' house soon. He left with the pair sticking out of his car trunk.

The sparrow was gone from the feeder and she was sorry she'd missed his leavetaking. She hoped he was all right.

But her desk was moved and she on-lined the library and settled in to make up for the lost hours.

The rain finally stopped and Nellie was aware of a sound she'd not heard for some days – not since the fall rains began. No. Not since cool summer mornings.

The birds were talking after the rain.

Nellie felt their sound was something more.

She opened the door to the porch and at the sound, birds spread buckshot – from below the porch, from the railings – to the fir tree or over the street. Nellie walked to the edge and looked down, and there was the sparrow, on the cement. She hurried down the stairs, out the front door. She knew without touching him that he was dead. She hunched over and could feel the tail of her skirt caught in a deep puddle. The fabric was heavy as she rocked forward to see the bird's eyes. His eyes were dull, though she knew they shouldn't be. He couldn't have been dead longer than perhaps three hours.

What was she to do? The other birds were filling fir and spruce with noise.

She tried to stand, but her left knee ached and she stayed

where she was. That was when Sebastian drove up, climbed out of his car, with hands of takeout bags.

'You killed one, did you?'

She tried again to stand. 'No call to be cheerful about it.'

He leaned over, turned the bird gently with his toe. 'Poor thing. You had him for a while, though.'

Nellie half-stood on one leg. Sebastian held out his hand to her, which she ignored as she straightened slowly.

'I didn't have him.'

'But you did.' He looked up at the feeder on the railing over their heads. 'You were blessed.'

Nellie stared down at the bird. She wouldn't have known him from any of the sparrows that visited.

'Why do you think he died?'

Sebastian bent closer. 'Salmonella poisoning, perhaps.' He was calm.

'Salmonella?' Nellie didn't want to crouch again. She was afraid her knee would never make it a second time.

'How often do you clean the floor of the feeder?'

What else did he know that he wasn't saying?

'It's all in that book I gave you. You did read it, didn't you?' His voice rose slightly and he reached into one of the bags and pulled out a deep-fried wonton. He held the bag out to her. Nellie shook her head. She had no interest in eating.

'Are you saying I poisoned this bird?'

'Could be,' he nodded. 'Don't take on now.'

What was *taking on*? Had her voice risen? If so, only to match his.

'Why didn't you tell me?'

He was standing, another wonton in his hand, and he had a strange look on his face. Nellie looked down to see if the buttons of her shirt were fastened.

He pulled a hand through his hair, and it peaked after a day of downtrodden work hours.

'I can't tell you everything.'

Nellie hadn't yelled in years. She didn't trust herself so she went into her home and sat at the kitchen table, away from the living room – though it was now hardly that – and away from the feeder.

And some time passed before she realized she'd left the bird and even as the thought passed through her mind, she heard a clunk of metal from out back and she went to the window to look. Sebastian was in his back yard with the light on and he had a shovel in his hand and was digging a hole in the grass. He moved the shovel in rhythmic arcs, as if he'd been digging that particular hole for some time now, though it was shallow and he'd opened the ground only seconds before. She watched as he lowered his hand in the hole for a moment before replacing the dirt and the bit of sod. The bird. He bent to press his hand against the earth and went quickly into his home without noticing her.

Who did he think he was? The bird was her responsibility – she would have taken care of him.

It was dark when she stepped out to bring the bird feeder in. She never should have done this. Why had she thought to build a feeder? She opened the front door just enough to push it through, and left it in the carport.

There was seed scattered over the balcony and on the ground below. For two days that fed the sparrows. The juncos stayed away and the chickadees.

On the third day there was silence. A waiting silence. A brief movement in the fir, a black head, grey chest, then gone.

Nellie rattled at her computer, made more coffee, pulled her socks off, rubbed her feet where she imagined them sore from sitting all day. Wished she'd left her desk where it was, upstairs, facing a wall.

Instead it was the window she faced, and what was outside of that window, and what she saw was empty. Her boxes of plants with all their life drawn in, into the twisted roots, like cantankerous shopkeepers setting out the Closed signs and drawing the blinds, leaving behind dead-brown for winter months. And the cold rain splatted down.

She was waiting again.

Down to the carport and she fetched the bloody thing, put it back in its place, caught the roar of Jaguar and remembered the dead sparrow. She took it up again and to the laundry, where she scrubbed with cold water and bleach. In her head she could hear Sebastian.

'Be quiet!' she cried out, and imagined a new stillness next door.

Back to the balcony, downstairs again to fetch the seed, and when she returned there was a flutter of grey-brown to the tree to safety. Their waiting she could live with.

Two handfuls, and she knew when she turned her back that they were there.

The next morning the juncos and the chickadees returned, and the next, a black and white and red bird sat astride the roof, curious.

It had to be a woodpecker, though Nellie couldn't remember ever having seen one. A downy woodpecker, with his red patch and white freckles, she found in the book. She took a sticky-backed notepaper, scribbled the date on it and affixed it to the page.

She spent the day reading Sebastian's mother's book, and note-taking.

Winter was coming. Seed was not enough. *Suet* – GO TO BUTCHER'S, she wrote – black oil sunflower seed, peanut butter, mixed fifty-fifty with cornmeal, broken dog biscuits, for chickadees. Dog biscuits. Chickadees. Really? *Raw apples, raisins, cut-up fruit, for waxwings.*

Waxwings. She looked it up in the index. Bohemian or cedar.

Cedar on the west coast.

Melted-butter bandits, she thought, as she looked at the photograph, the rounded-smooth body, the black mask. *Imagine one of those in my world,* she thought.

October was cold and Nellie wore her cardigan always, and early November there was ice and that silence that means snow.

The butcher gave her chunks of suet. 'Render it,' he said, 'And it won't go bad.'

Nellie read the book, and rendered, mixed the suet with seed, set it out.

Sebastian heard her on the porch and came through his doors with a small box. 'Grit,' he said. 'Broken seashells. They need it this time of year.' He turned away.

'Good of you to tell me,' said Nellie and her voice was loud. She couldn't recall reading about grit in the book.

'You're welcome,' he said.

Her voice was louder. 'I don't remember thanking you.'

'You're going to frighten the birds.'

'Fuck the birds!'

'They don't.'

She was amusing him. She was sure. 'Don't laugh at me.'

He leaned over the railing. 'I'm not laughing at you!'

How was it possible to yell without anger? she wondered after him.

She buttoned her sweater before she went in, and when she was in, she found a scarf she wound several times around her neck and shoulders. It was brown and black, like a fall night, and warmed her. The box of grit she placed on her desk for the morning. She would read about it first. She must have missed it in the book.

The next morning the wood floor was colder and she slipped long johns under her skirt before heading downstairs. She was expecting a file, and she huddled over the fax machine and blew on her hands. The file had not come. Coffee then, and the window while waiting. She crouched at the heat duct by the French door and was startled to see the wide back of some bird, whose head reached almost to the roof of the feeder. She fingered her own scarf when she saw his brown and black chevron stripes. He turned crookedly and she saw a flash of red at his neck as he poked at the suet, and her skirt filled with air warm from the duct.

Sebastian chose that moment to step out onto his deck, and the bird was away.

'You scared him!' She called out even before she'd opened the door.

Sebastian knew what she was saying.

'Don't yell at me!' His hair stood morning-up.

'Don't frighten my birds.'

'Are you going to curse at me again?' He was actually grinning.

'I might.'

'I've waited a long time for you to care. Do you know what that bird was?'

There was a loud cry from across the street, in the maple, almost a crow sound.

'A northern flicker.'

Another cry swallowed his next words, but Nellie caught something about grit. 'Grit yourself,' she said.

'Nitty-gritty,' he said.

Caw. Except the sound was more like *keeeer.*

There was an answer close by, but Nellie didn't see them until later, at dusk. Something blue and dark-crested and there were two. One landed at the feeder, played with the suet, called to the other, shimmying the tree. The second one waited for the first to move, then came and scattered seed over the porch. Both laughed and Nellie felt a sharp pain low in her belly.

[136]

Page 276. Stellar's Jays. She tucked the book inside her vest and went next door to show Sebastian.

Somebody's Steed

EILIS KEPT HER HAIR LONG and coiled to her head with some tortoiseshell bit clinging to it because damn it all, she was a woman. If her appearance fooled people who knew her, or thought they knew her, well, that was their problem. Look at Marianne Faithfull: she wasn't afraid of appearing in public, looking like a librarian was supposed to, in gray flannel jumpsuit, and singing about her snatch.

Eilis had hoped though that with menopause, her hair would thin, but no. (Annie called it her tresses, and said she would have liked to have them herself.) It still took twenty minutes to wash and all day to dry. It was a twice-weekly ritual. Annie would help her comb it. Or she used to.

Eilis imagined being able to hang her hair on the clothesline, combing through tangles with the garden rake, until each strand was free and could move with the wind on its own beside the others. There was some chestnut left – that's what the generous ones used to call it. In the sunlight you'd even swear there was some red. And lots of white shining. 'I'm no prince,' she told Annie. 'But with these legs, I could be somebody's steed.'

'Carry me away,' Annie would say.

'Don't go yet,' Eilis said. She wasn't ready for Annie to die. She wished Annie would fight just a little more so she could remember her that way, and feel loved.

Not that she didn't feel loved. But there were times when she couldn't allow herself to feel so.

The neighbours knew something was afoot, even though Annie and Eilis sold one car, so that there wouldn't be two sitting in the drive. (Eilis took a leave of absence from work; their savings would be gone, but what was money? Old single women lived at poverty level in a number that she could be added to, unnoticed.)

'On holiday?' Mr Saunders asked. Eilis felt that he was always watching them from next door. She knew it couldn't be; he must have things to do. But it did seem that most of those things were yard work – mostly on their side of his yard. No, that was her imagination. Really, the poor fellow had a miserable marriage; that was why he was out-of-doors so much. Even in the rain. 'One could garden year round in this part of the country,' he'd told her. 'Now when we lived in Fredericton ...' he'd begun, but Eilis interrupted. Told him she'd lived in Halifax, in Brandon, in Edmonton. She was careful not to say 'we'. She was always careful about that. It was too easy; say 'we' and the listener's eyebrows went up in interest. Not idle curiosity, but genuine interest. People really did want to know. So Eilis never made that mistake.

Other people said it so easily. 'We went to Palm Springs,' and Eilis could see it: the speaker, a woman, shopping with a sizeable tote over a sloping shoulder, her partner, encapped and stewing over the exchange rate on the rental of a golf cart. Or the speaker was a younger woman. 'We went to Disneyland,' and Eilis could see that, too. A diaper bag full of Wet-Ones, and cameras – still and video – tickets and brochures, one kid still in a stroller, the oldest muttering about going home and missing sports day.

She shouldn't do it, she told herself: play those reels ... it was those pictures in her own mind that caused her to fear the pictures in the minds of others.

'No, Mr Saunders. I'm not on holiday. Just taking time off from work.'

'Oh,' he said, and paused, or so it seemed to Eilis.

'Annie, too?' he asked, after raking the grass around his feet into a neat pile. 'I see her in the sun porch in the middle of the day lately. My Dorothy says she misses her at the Sewing Corner.'

'Annie has decided to leave her job. Early retirement,' she added, wishing she could escape.

But Mr Saunders had wrapped his hands over the end of his rake. 'I see that developer fellow is after you, too, the presumptuous little bastard.'

That was a new tone for Mr Saunders.

'He's not a particularly tall man, is he,' said Eilis.

Mr Saunders snorted.

'He wants our land, doesn't he. Probably for some bloody string of little box houses planted in cement.' He scratched with his rake at a bit of grass he'd missed. 'Nothing grows in cement,' he growled.

'You're so angry,' Eilis said.

He looked at her, startled. 'You aren't thinking of selling, are you?'

'No, of course not.'

'I mean, it's not like you have family here and all, but it is your home.'

'It is my home,' she echoed, and fought the quick lump in her throat.

'When I go' – he motioned to the sky – 'I don't want to leave my Dorothy in some strange place. I want to leave her here, with the garden, where we've been, where our children have walked. It's where she's comfortable, where she wants to be.'

So Eilis had been mistaken about the man's marriage. 'You think you'll be the first to go, do you?'

'Men don't live long in my family.' He paused, then, 'Well,' he said, turning to go, 'don't let that bastard grind you down.'

Eilis and Annie lived in what would have been dismissed as a slough shack, a one-bedroom, wartime bungalow – their fox-hole, Annie called it – on the original main street of the town, backing onto the slough, a stream of slow-moving brown water, most appreciated by ducks. (The town was a place of ten thousand at the most. Small enough that marriage engage-ment notices – with photos – were posted in the local paper.) The street was winding and guarded by elms and Japanese maples and other trees that had never wanted to call the lower mainland their home. Still they grew in the coastal damp, big-ger than they could possibly grow elsewhere, and the town council and the people argued about cutting them down.

Eilis and Annie had bought the property for the garden, for the willow trailing into the water, for the rich mossy bank. They'd thought to tear down the little house, build anew. But no. They'd rewired, insulated, painted, put in a wood-burning stove, added a sun porch, and left the old tea roses growing up the side. The garden surrounded the house, wide and green, protecting.

Across the street was a house with a picture window. A window that caused Eilis to think of Woodward's department store, downtown in the city when she was a girl. Such decora-tion.

When Annie was first diagnosed there'd been silken autumn leaves on fine threads, filling the window with their artificial dying colour. Two weeks later there was a great cor-nucopia, with squashes, pumpkins, apples – golden and red – spilling out. Eilis had seen family trooping up the stairs for dinner. (Her mother had warned her she'd regret not having children.)

She and Annie had eaten Cornish hen that day. Annie wasn't very hungry. Eilis had already learned to place a mor-sel surrounded by colour on a plate, so fine that Annie couldn't pass; she still knew Annie's weak spots. And two of

Annie's girls came over: girls from the high school just down the road and around the corner. Another reason to keep her profile flattened; Annie enjoyed her volunteer work at the school. The school had an after-hours program (keep the kids busy until the parents are home), and Annie handled the arts projects. For Annie, that meant using all the scraps and bolt ends from the store where she worked. The things those kids dreamed up with fabric stiffener, stuffing material, and odd buttons: simple appliqué, taken home for the walls, and life-size works that must have had parents sputtering about their living rooms and entrance halls. The art wasn't exactly hang-on-the-fridge work. The work of the kids was what made Annie's job at the local sewing store worthwhile.

'Find something, too,' she told Eilis.

'When I'm retired, I'll travel,' Eilis would say.

'How conventional,' Annie said, though not unkindly.

'Conventional,' said Eilis. 'I've worked in a bank since I graduated from high school. Maybe I should buy golf clubs.'

Annie giggled. 'Oh, don't. You might kill someone with one.'

Last year Annie's students' work had been displayed at the municipal hall. One piece – made of zippers, and symbolic of nineties sexuality – had been removed; offensive, some tax-payer called it. There was a glut of letters to the paper. Both sides, certainly, but the words left Annie feeling that she'd best keep her fig leaves in place.

Annie'd been miserable in high school. Lonely. Unlike Eilis, she'd never had anything to do with a boy. Somehow – it wasn't anything she ever said – the young students she worked with sensed that misery; it was like their own. They were drawn to her. It wasn't unusual for Eilis to come home from work and find several in the backyard, cigarettes in hand, their feet in the slough; two in the kitchen making tea; one curled by the bookshelf, turning pages.

Eilis hadn't seen one since the diagnosis, but Thanksgiving brought them back. Slowly, in twos, was how they could deal with it.

'Do you ever tell them?' Eilis had once asked Annie. Before they knew Annie was ill.

'No. I don't need to. They know, and they know I accept them as they are.'

'Sappho.'

Annie accepted the name with a smile.

But after the Thanksgiving meal, when the two visitors (with their bright red, newly coloured hair) had left, Annie wondered. 'Maybe it wouldn't have hurt to say something now and again. In case they had some doubt. How much can be unsaid? I've just been so afraid of being found out. In this place where they take children's books from library shelves.'

The man representing the developing company was young and carried himself with a great supply of business cards. *Ken McDonough* was the name on the rich textured paper. *Living Developments.*

'Have you considered selling?'

Eilis had never liked standing in an open doorway talking, but she didn't want to invite the man in. They didn't have a hallway; it would have meant standing in the middle of their living room, and she didn't want him there. So they stood with the door wide open.

The man's gaze shifted and Eilis turned to see Annie standing for a moment in the kitchen doorway, her arms holding her red robe around her. Her legs were thin; she'd lost so much weight already.

'I apologize,' he said – Eilis guessed that he was talking to her. 'I assumed you were the owner.'

'I am,' she said. 'And no. I don't want to sell.'

'You may want to look at this,' he said, and pressed a thin

folder into her hand. She was glad to close the door behind him.

Annie was resting on the chaise lounge in the sun porch. She put her hand out for the folder. She opened it, studied the contents for a moment. Eilis poured coffee. 'They want it badly,' said Annie. 'They have next door, the Clipshams' place.'

'They haven't even lived there for almost a year. Tumbledown shack.'

'I'll miss the blackberries. I suppose they'll rip them out. They've been so handy, next door.'

Eilis nodded. 'They make the best cobbler.'

'Though the seeds do go through me. Don't suppose I could eat some now.'

They were quiet, in thought, Eilis looking out the window. Through the hanging branches of the willow you could see, on the other side of the slough, the parking lot of the local mall. Eilis was always glad for summer, and the green that almost hid the cars.

She laughed suddenly. Annie looked frightened. 'What? What is it?

'Us,' Eilis said. 'Out there, picking blackberries. We must have looked like pest-control experts in our gum boots and leather gloves, those wretched old ski jackets, the nylon fabric pulling and popping on the thorns.'

Annie relaxed, laughed too. 'How we could shovel the berries off the branches and into our buckets and bowls. Remember the time we filled twelve in half an hour?'

'No! We weren't that fast!'

'We were. Half an hour. Enough for one winter.'

'But we went back for more.'

'Seems to me we were sick that night. We ate too many.'

'We were sick.'

Radiation, though the doctor advised against it (later, Eilis would realize they'd done the radiation for her, and not for Annie at all) and Hallowe'en loomed across the street. In the picture window, there were ghosts and glowing skulls. A witch in black with a wig rescued from the seventies.

'She's bald under that, you know,' Annie murmured. She scared Eilis, coming up beside her, so quietly that Eilis didn't know she was there until she spoke.

Eilis didn't like what played through her mind when Annie said *bald*. 'She's Styrofoam, too,' she added, nodding at the witch.

'But she'll be back in the window next year.'

Eilis had to speak quickly. 'I'd give you mine if I could.' She rested her chin on Annie's shoulder, and wrapped her hair gently around Annie's neck. Annie put a hand into Eilis's thick hair. Their fingers met, and Annie leaned against her.

Eilis was glad the neighbour forgot Remembrance Day.

For Christmas there were lights everywhere. Coloured lights, and those twinkly white lights everyone had taken to. (Then they'd leave them up all year.) And a white angel on the roof, with golden cords crossing between her breasts and winding around her waist, and a full gown of white, yellow hair in waves down her shoulders. She was too big, with an amazing wing span. At night, there was a spotlight on her.

'Jesus,' said Annie when she saw her. '*She* didn't fly in on a broom.'

They decided that the house across the street was enough; they didn't need a tree of their own. But on Christmas Eve their minds began to turn. Even with the curtains closed, they could see the neighbours' lights, red, green and blue, shining over the top of the curtain in an odd across-the-ceiling pattern, something like a kite tail.

'I suppose we could have had something green,' Annie said.

'Why did we decide not to? Tell me again.'

'I don't remember,' Annie said.

Eilis didn't remind her that it was she – Annie – who had suggested they not have a tree. The cutting of a live thing seemed to bother her. 'How about an artificial one?' Eilis had asked. But no. 'An artificial one isn't the same,' she said.

It was after ten o'clock.

'It's late,' Annie said. She crossed the room – Eilis could see pain in her slow steps – and pulled an afghan from the back of the chesterfield. 'It's cold.'

'I could do that,' said Eilis.

Annie wrapped the afghan around her shoulders before sitting again in her chair. 'I'll ask you when I need you,' she said softly. 'It bothers me when you bustle over me, when you leap about. I know how you love me.'

Even as she heard Annie's words, Eilis fought the urge to move from her chair. She lost.

'Where are you going now?' Annie called to her, there in the coat closet, wrangling her heavy denim jacket from a wire hanger.

'I won't be long,' Eilis said, her thoughts ahead of her: there was a saw in the toolshed; there was a scrubby pine by the side fence.

She set her saw to the tree, but couldn't. The thought of Annie in the house stopped her. She stood. Strange how moonlight always changed the familiar. No wonder people loved by moonlight.

Next door, the old Clipsham place was empty and dark, boards hanging from the back windows where kids had gone in, to get away. Eilis walked slowly along the side of the house to the front, her feet sinking deep into the thick grass. The large plywood development sign, with its numbered squares and explanations, was ugly. The cut-off cedar hedge – to allow room for the sign – was ugly. The old wrought iron fence was ugly. The gate had come off its hinges and had been flung aside. Eilis had seen the young Mr McDonough do that. He'd cursed the thing and left it.

Eilis looked at the gate at her feet. It was probably as old as the town. These houses along the slough were among the first. The gate had a series of spikes along the top, rising into a peak, and curlicues over its customary vertical bars. Iron ivy leaves decorated the curlicues, though many of the leaves had long come off. It was heavy, but it wasn't impossible. She carried it home.

Annie sat and watched while Eilis set the gate between bricks on the coffee table. (They'd often talked of getting rid of that table; it was a large square, too large for the room, but it gracefully held the gate.)

'A dark gate,' Annie said under her breath. Then she was quiet while Eilis collected candles from the kitchen drawer, the bedside table, the box on the ledge behind the wood stove. Eilis lit a candle and melted the bases of the others over the flame, then pushed the soft wax onto the iron. The old gate glowed, and shadows danced on the walls and spread over the ceiling. The neighbours' kite-tail colour disappeared.

'Not so dark,' Annie said when she was done.

Eilis made hot rum, and they put their feet up on the table, and watched the candles burn, watched the wax drip over the ivy leaves, the square bars. Annie fell asleep in her chair.

The room was silent except for her breathing.

Eilis stayed in her chair. That was it then: their last Christmas Eve; their last closing of a calendar year. She'd always imagined Annie and herself getting old – when I'm sixty-four will you still love me – old enough so that they didn't have to be so careful. People wouldn't question two old women living together as they would two younger women. She'd imagined a house of books and plants and fat satisfied cats, and the two of them with thick pyjamas over loose skin.

Annie'd always said they should be proud of who they were. But that was as far as she went. She said, 'We know who we are. We know what we have,' and Eilis agreed. It was personal, it was precious – and it would be so long as they had it between them. 'So long as you both shall live.'

It was all the other stuff: people at work trying to set up blind dates; financial experts asking about spousal benefits; ancient relatives making inquiries. (At least now they were past menopause and free of that last one.)

Annie had wanted a child; that came back to Eilis now, in the silence of a holiday eve. Why had they decided not to? For a moment, Eilis imagined ... what would such a child be now? Thirteen? Fourteen? She almost choked with the thought of an adolescent sharing their home. Funny. They'd talked and talked about a baby, but she'd never once envisioned a teenager. And it would go on: a student, home for the weekend from university ... Eilis felt short of breath imagining an adult child. An emissary, traveling with head up, a new generation.... No, that was what she'd been afraid of: child as political experiment.

The last candle was out suddenly. Smoke trailed across the room. The smell of wax was heavy, sedating. It was the hour when absolutely everyone else was asleep. They might have been dead.

A great coldness was in Eilis.

For months now they'd been living with the idea of Annie's death. The cancer was spreading so rapidly. Bones, blood. But that was the first time that Eilis had felt such cold, graveside cold. It wrapped around her and brought her sleep, in her chair, like a traveler.

Annie died on January 6, at home.

On the twelfth day of Christmas my true love gave to me twelve lords a-leaping. The day the green is to come down.

The neighbours didn't know about Annie when they chose that day to pull their lights from their eaves. Eilis imagined them beginning their preparations for Valentine's Day. All the bloody saints and their holidays. Such ritual. Tradition. For so many years she'd sat in her corner, hating convention. Fearing. And with that fear, respect. Grudging. But respect. She hadn't moved from her corner.

Widowhood. The word struck out at her.

It was something else she'd never thought of: such a word belonging to her, but of course it did. She could pull it down in front of her like a spring-rolled blind and hide behind it.

But she'd have to keep it to herself, wouldn't she?

The bitterness swept through her – she didn't know where from – and almost knocked her to her feet. It was so big, so poisonous.

Her grandmother had assumed widowhood. Eilis remembered her black clothes, and boxes and boxes of coloured clothing being sent away, her mother helping to pack them up. Always after her husband's death, Eilis's grandmother had seemed drab, grey, but her greyness had been accepted, expected even. And she'd died two years later. No one was surprised.

Eilis's mother had been different. Fifteen years earlier, and Eilis could remember her mother at her husband's funeral. The stoic. Such straight lines about her. Her back, crossed by the line of her shoulders, her feet long and flat. Stick person. And at the graveside, not a tear. It had seemed so very wrong to Eilis, yet her mother had been so proud. 'I must keep it together,' she'd said. 'He would expect me to.'

But would he want you to? Eilis had wondered. Still wondered as she stood over her sink, eating crackers and cheese. It didn't seem worthwhile fixing a meal and eating at the table.

On the other side of the street, the neighbours believed in red velvet. Yards of it in the window. Two cupids flying across the plush, and hearts hanging from the branches of the tree in the middle of the yard. At night a red spotlight. And balloons, red, white, and silver.

'Wonderful view,' Mr McDonough joked. 'I can see why you don't want to sell.' He'd taken to loosening his tie the last two visits, and that day the sun was shining so he took off his jacket. For the friendly approach, Eilis guessed.

He didn't know Annie had died; he'd gotten over his first thought – that she was the homeowner – and he'd probably come to the conclusion that Annie was a guest.

So he tried the single-woman tack: 'This is the most you'll ever be offered for this piece of land. With this kind of money you can buy a beautiful condo, or a cozy place in a gated community. A safe place. And you can vacation in California every year. Have a nest egg. Can you afford to say no?'

'I wonder if I could charge you with harassment? Or stalking? Which do you think would apply?'

He lifted his brows.

'Go,' Eilis said. She closed the door.

The bank called her. Asked her how she was feeling, when she was coming back. 'A close friend of mine has died,' she said.

'Oh, I'm so sorry to hear that. Do you need to extend your leave of absence? Is the funeral out of town?'

'No – my friend lived close by.'

There was silence. The bank, waiting.

'I'll call you back,' said Eilis at last.

Eilis walked through the clustering of stores that formed the town core, to the newspaper office. She never had written an obituary. Annie had told her that she did not want a service.

'A Valentine's Day message?' said the woman at the desk,

her hands over the keyboard. 'Spell the name, please.'

'A-N-N-I-E.' She began to spell her surname, and stopped. 'Just Annie. In loving memory.'

'Your name?' The woman at the desk droned.

Eilis didn't answer. She opened her wallet. 'I'll pay cash.' She put the money on the desk.

Then the woman looked at her, and Eilis fled.

In the park, she sat under a dying pear tree in the cold winter sun.

It wasn't enough.

Mr McDonough stayed away, but she knew he was near. The bulldozer took the Clipshams' place; the hammers started in. The bank sent a letter; she didn't respond.

There were white bunnies in the branches across the street, and baskets; eggs, blue, purple, pink, yellow, hanging, hanging everywhere.

The hours after supper were beginning to stretch with daylight. Eilis had rather liked the respite of darkness, but it was no longer hers.

A knock came one evening. Two of Annie's girls, scared. 'We saw your memory in the paper,' one said. The other kept her eyes fixed on the construction next door and took quick puffs from her cigarette.

Eilis motioned them in. 'Tea?'

The girl who spoke said, 'Yes,' and Eilis set the kettle on the stove.

They both looked around curiously, but were quiet.

Eilis tried to make conversation. 'How are your art classes?'

'We haven't gone this year. Not since September.'

The other girl continued puffing.

Not since Annie was there, thought Eilis. Annie had taught a few classes at the beginning of the school year.

'Miss Gilchrist said she'd do it,' the girl went on.

The other stood abruptly and began to search for something. Eilis didn't know where Annie would have kept the ashtray. The girl gave up after opening the obvious cupboards, and went out the kitchen door. Eilis became aware that both she and the talking girl were watching these actions and not speaking. The other girl returned, slammed the screen door behind her. 'Gilchrist has bird shit on her shoulder, and she doesn't even know it.' She sat down.

'She's not Annie,' agreed the other. Paula, her name was, when she introduced herself. 'And this is Rand.' Rand nodded, and began to dig for another cigarette.

'Annie left a lot of stuff at the school, in the studio. We thought maybe you'd want it.'

Eilis started to shake her head, and stopped. 'Maybe,' she said.

Rand stood. 'The school's open.'

Paula explained. 'Rand's not happy sitting.'

'But it's almost seven o'clock,' Eilis said.

'Night school,' Rand said simply.

The janitor unlocked the studio door, and Rand led the way to a storage space in the furthest corner of the room. Fabric spilled out of the shelves. Half-finished projects tumbled from the walls. Rand moved forward and pulled something from the garbage can. 'Bloody Gilchrist,' she said. It was a twisted shape, small pieces of wood nailed and glued. Eilis couldn't see what it was really, until Paula pointed out. 'That was Trish's baby she was making.' She took it from her friend's hands. Then Eilis could see it: the arms reaching out, the face upturned. There were other forms, similar. 'What are these?' she asked.

'We were working on a set of children.' Paula pulled one from the mess of forms. 'This is yours, isn't it, Rand?'

'Yeah.'

'She's all folded up.'

'She's kneeling, she's listening.'

'Is Miss Gilchrist really going to throw this away?' Eilis wanted to gather all those wooden bones and take them home. 'What were you going to do with them?'

Rand shrugged, and dropped hers onto the floor. Several boards came loose.

Eilis decided. 'Do you think the janitor will notice if we take this?'

'We can put it out the window,' Paula said.

'I'll bring around the car,' said Eilis.

The living room was filled. The hour was late. Rand had found the ashtray, but had perhaps reconsidered her smoke; she stood in the doorway, the door open.

There were wooden shapes and extra scraps, bolts of fabric, stuffing, an old dressmaker's form made of strips of brown paper. Eilis thought she recognized it from the sewing store. The owner had probably given it to Annie; there was a tremendous hole in one side, and the legs were crushed. Still, Annie had probably had plans for her.

'Your neighbours are nuts,' said Paula, beside Rand at the door. 'What's the deal with the Easter stuff?'

'Every holiday they decorate.' Eilis stood behind her. She stepped out into the yard. A car passed down the street. Mr McDonough. He waved. She turned away to see Mr Saunders waving at the man. Her house looked smaller when she looked back at it.

'Let's put them on the roof,' she said to Paula, and to Rand. 'The children.' They nodded.

They worked all night, wrapping stuffing and fabric in

place, painting faces with fabric paint. For clothing, they wound fabric around the little bodies, tied bright sashes. The girls climbed the ladder to the roof; Eilis could hear their steps overhead. They used flashlights to find a crevice in the chimney: a place to hang a trouble light. She could hear their voices discussing where each child might sit or stand. Then up and down the ladder, while Eilis swathed the dress form with a white sheet, draped a blue shawl over the figure. Somehow she didn't like the head covered. She handed her up to Paula and Rand. 'How about if she sits – I'll get a crate.' She cut into the sides of a crate so that it would sit over the ridge pole.

In the morning the sun rose over an odd grouping on the rooftop: a circle of children gathered around a figure in white and blue, long hair waving in the wind. Hair mostly silver, a touch of red. Generous people would even say chestnut.

Alison Acheson is the author of two juvenile/young adult novels – *The Half-Pipe Kidd* (Coteau Books, 1997) and *Thunder Ice* (Coteau Books, 1996). The latter has been short-listed for the Geoffrey Bilson Award for historical fiction, the Red Cedar Award and the Manitoba Young Reader Award. Her stories have been published in *The New Quarterly*, *Grain* and *Antigonish Review*.

Alison has an MFA in creative writing and a degree in history from UBC. She lives in Ladner, B.C. with her husband and two sons.